Every moment Richard spends with Ellen makes him realize how much he has grown to care for her—and reminds him of why he must leave her alone.

Richard realized his wayward hand had caressed Ellen's back as he held her. Even now, as she looked up at him with questioning eyes, her face was so close to his, lifted to his own—how easy it would be. . .how easy. . .

He became aware of himself as a man holding a woman, a soft, warm, appealing woman. For an instant, the moment had become something other than a boss consoling his employee, a man consoling a woman. He wanted to give in to the growing feelings in his heart and pursue a relationship with her. But that included revealing things that he'd tried to put behind him. How much did a person have to reveal about the past?

Acceptance had not come easy for him. He'd given that situation from his past to God but kept taking it back. He'd lost respect for himself. He didn't want to lose Ellen's respect.

He moved back, lest she detect the increase in his heart rate. *Get hold of yourself, Richard. You know better than to let this happen.*

Had Ellen wondered about his hasty retreat? She turned and held onto the railing. No, her mind wasn't on him at all. His shouldn't have been on her. He sat in his chair, forcing his thoughts back to the issue at hand.

YVONNE LEHMAN, an award-winning novelist, lives in the heart of North Carolina's Smoky Mountains. She has four grown children and several grandchildren. In addition to being an inspirational romance writer, she is also the founder of the Blue Ridge Christian Writers' Conference.

Books by Yvonne Lehman

HEARTSONG PRESENTS

Don't miss out on any of our super romances. Write to us at the following address for information on our newest releases and club information.

Heartsong Presents Readers' Service
PO Box 719
Uhrichsville, OH 44683

Or visit www.heartsongpresents.com

On a Clear Day

Yvonne Lehman

Heartsong Presents

With loving gratitude to Lori and Lisa for their invaluable comments on my work.

Jesus said to the people, "I am the light of the world.
If you follow me, you won't be stumbling through the
darkness, because you will have the light that leads to life."
JOHN 8:12 NLT

A note from the Author:
I love to hear from my readers! You may correspond
with me by writing:

Yvonne Lehman
Author Relations
PO Box 719
Uhrichsville, OH 44683

ISBN 1-58660-668-9

ON A CLEAR DAY

All Scripture quotations, unless otherwise indicated, are taken from
the HOLY BIBLE, NEW INTERNATIONAL VERSION ®. NIV®. Copyright ©
1973, 1978, 1984 by International Bible Society. Used by permission
of Zondervan Publishing House. All rights reserved.

PRINTED IN THE U.S.A.

one

"I can't have you working here anymore. I'm going to have to let you go."

Ellen Jonsen winced as a crash of thunder echoed through the mountains. Her glance darted to the window where hard rain pelted the small panes and blurred the landscape. A streak of lightning split the sky with the same tearing force Patsy Hatcher's words were having on Ellen's heart.

Ellen's gaze returned to the grim-faced director of the Little Tykes Preschool. "What did you say?"

Patsy opened a manila file that lay on the desk in front of her. "Ellen Jonsen" was written on the tab. Patsy drew out a piece of paper. "It's another complaint about your proselytizing."

"But I haven't—"

Patsy's uplifted hand stopped Ellen's words. "Did you, or did you not, invite Janice Sims and her daughter Judy to your church?"

Ellen had no reason to deny that. "Well, yes, after Missy told Judy about the Kid's Club and Judy said she'd like to go. I told Janice about the program. That's all."

Patsy tapped the folder. "That was done on these premises."

"And Janice complained?" That was unbelievable. She'd seemed interested.

"No, not Janice." Patsy's glare held accusation. "You were overheard."

Overheard? That had to be one of the workers who often spouted her "tolerant" attitude. Tolerance—except for Christians. "You mean someone eavesdropped on my private conversation, then complained?"

"Your private conversations tend to be very public." Patsy's clipped tone stung. "This is not the first time, Ellen."

5

Ellen felt as if she'd suddenly become a little preschooler, being reprimanded for pushing a child and causing him to fall. "After you told me not to mention my faith, I stopped." That had been against her deepest feelings and against what the Lord expected of His followers.

"Oh, Ellen. Now tell the truth."

Ellen felt heat rise to her face. *Now I'm being accused of lying?*

Patsy didn't let up. This remarkable senior citizen, whom Ellen admired, had become her enemy. "You're always talking about what's going on at your church. You and Heather talk about Jesus as if He's your best friend. We all hear it. Even the children." Her shoulders straightened as she leaned back against her chair. "That's where I have to draw the line. We will not allow one person's religious beliefs to be taken as what we represent here." She leaned forward, her forearms resting on the folder. "We're not a church. We're a school."

Ellen felt as steady as the oak tree outside the window, whose branches swayed to and fro in the wind. Was there no getting through to this woman? She thought not, so why not speak her mind?

"Patsy, you all talk about the movies you see. The music you listen to. What you hear on TV. What's in the newspaper. Whatever is going on around you." She took a deep breath. "Why can't I talk about what's important to me?"

"Others hear when you talk about it to Heather, who is writing her master's thesis about this school. I'm aware that theses can be published as articles or books." Patsy stood.

Ellen wondered if she were having a nightmare. How could a person change so? This white-haired woman had represented a grandmotherly figure to her, had been her mentor in child care. Now, her tall slender presence loomed over her like a threat.

Patsy's lips formed a stern line. "The reputation of this school is at stake. I will not have it represented as a religious organization." She sighed. "Ellen, religion is not something you force on another person. It's private and personal. Especially around children."

Ellen gasped. "I would never—"

"Ah!" Patsy lifted a finger. "At lunchtime were you, or were you not, singing 'Jesus Loves Me' to Missy? And don't you think other children could hear that?"

"Missy was afraid of the storm, and I was comforting her. Patsy, she's my own child."

"Your own child?" Patsy scoffed. "That's not true, Ellen."

Accused of lying again.

Ellen swallowed hard. "It's true in the ways that count. In my heart."

If ever Ellen had heard a condescending tone, it was when Patsy walked around the desk and came close. "Maybe other things in your heart aren't true either, Ellen. Like your opinion of how everybody else can get to God."

❧

I'm. . .fired!

Ellen repeated the statement to herself several times after Patsy left the office. Ellen sat alone, no longer aware of the storm outside. A great calm, like the calm at the center of a hurricane, enclosed her.

Patsy didn't want her to work a notice.

If she had quit, she'd be required to give a two-week notice.

Patsy didn't even want her to stay to tell the final story of the day. The children loved that. What would they think? What would the other workers think?

Ellen didn't have time to explain to anyone. Too numb for tears, she told herself she could handle this. But what would it do to Missy?

Missy had adjusted so well—had taken a sense of pride in Ellen's telling the stories.

Do I take Missy home now? She'll wonder why I'm not telling the story.

Should I say I'll be back for her later?

Should I let Missy continue in the preschool?

Ellen did not believe Patsy would ever mistreat Missy. She was not a terrible person. On the contrary, she was competent and well-organized. Ellen had never doubted Patsy's commitment to the welfare of those children. Patsy hired only the most capable, dedicated workers. They were wonderful. Heather would be there for awhile longer too. That was positive.

Numb from having been fired, Ellen wondered if this were some kind of nightmare. She walked from the office and down the hallway, glass windows along the outer wall on her right, being pounded by heavy rain.

Since her mom's unexpected death two years earlier, Ellen's emotions had stayed near the surface. And what had just happened was no small thing. She felt as if her world had collapsed again, bringing to mind the wall that had collapsed on her mom's car parked in a lot near the department store where she had worked. Mom wasn't the only one killed that day. Two workers on scaffolds and three other people in the car next to her mom's lost their lives as well. They'd gotten in their cars to go home. They'd never made it.

Struggling for control, Ellen stopped for a moment and placed her hand on the cool window pane.

Taking a deep breath, she gazed at the rivulets of water obscuring what lay beyond the windows. But the scenery was imprinted upon her mind. An immaculate green lawn spread out in front of the long white building on which cartoon characters had been painted. Atop the roof hung a huge sign announcing Little Tykes Preschool. The sign included wooden characters depicting little boys and girls. A girl with golden braids jumped rope. A dark-haired boy pulled a wagon in which two other children rode. A child held a teddy bear. A boy read a book.

The appearance of the school had attracted Ellen.

So had Patsy Hatcher, no stranger to hard work.

Ellen had been impressed with Patsy's reasons for having a school, rather than simply a day-care center. Patsy had been a principal at a primary school and saw firsthand that so many children weren't prepared to leave home and go off to a full day at school. Many were traumatized. She wanted to provide a means of preparation for children.

Many people whose advice Ellen had sought confirmed that Little Tykes had the best reputation around and advised that getting Missy into a program where she could relate to other children would be good for her.

Ellen had never doubted that God had led her to Little Tykes and the job that allowed her to spend the days with Missy, whose little life had been turned upside down.

Now, Ellen wondered if she had failed God. She'd messed up what had seemed like such a perfect solution to earning a living while having time to be involved with Missy. Had she really been so overbearing about her faith? She didn't think so. But Patsy did.

God, don't let me fall apart right here. Give me strength and the kind of peace only You can give in the midst of trials.

She took a deep breath and turned to continue down the hall. On her left against the solid wall, red, orange, green, and yellow raincoats and umbrellas hung on pegs low enough for children to reach. Ellen passed the closed door with a big "2" on it, then a "3." Colorful baskets for the children formed a neat rainbow across the floor.

Ellen stood for a moment at the door with a big red "4" on it. Missy took pride in reading the numbers and finding her own room. The cold doorknob in Ellen's hand mimicked a spot in her heart. For two years, this had been a big part of her life.

I don't work here anymore.

A deep breath preceded her turning the knob, opening the door, and stepping inside the room onto the green carpet—the color of grass in the summertime. The big round smiley-face clock on the far wall indicated the time was 1:05 P.M. Five minutes past the time for the final story of the day.

There would be no story, except the one she'd tell Missy. And her dad. And Heather. And her friends. Patsy stood to one side, talking to Heather.

Some workers walked past with wet finger-painted pictures to be hung to dry on wooden racks in the hall. Others herded the little ones into the bathroom to wash their hands. Missy and several other children had already parked themselves on the floor, facing the chair where Ellen normally told the story that was in a picture book she'd hold up for them to see.

Patsy walked past without a glance.

Heather came over to the children. "Instead of a story today you're going to see a movie. *The Lion King*. Any of you seen that?"

Amid the clamor of children responding with arms lifted high, hands waving, "Yea's," and clapping, Ellen's gaze met Heather's questioning one.

Ellen gave a simple shake of her head. She retrieved her purse from a cabinet, then walked over to Missy and touched her shoulder. "Come on, Honey. We have to go."

Missy looked up, her blond curls bouncing against her cheeks as she spoke emphatically. "It's not time. We get to see *The Lion King*."

Beginning to feel the full impact of the situation, Ellen blinked back the moisture threatening her eyes. Little children and workers looked her way. Was Patsy standing like a warden at the door?

"Come on. We have to go, Honey. I'll tell you why later. You can watch *The Lion King* at home."

Missy's voice and eyes pleaded. "I want to see it here."

"I'm sorry. Not today. Now come on."

Reluctantly, Missy rose to her feet. She glanced at a friend. "I have to go. Bye." She waved her little hand to some who looked at her.

The soundtrack marked the introduction to *The Lion King* and the dismissal of Ellen. She couldn't even say good-bye to the children. She looked around. Their attention focused on the TV. A few workers stared at Ellen and Missy.

Ellen could hardly believe Patsy would allow the children to watch a video. On very few occasions did they watch TV, then only an educational program. Normally, there would be interactive activities. Obviously, Patsy was quite upset.

At the doorway, lightening flashed and thunder crashed. Missy jumped, squealed, and wrapped her arms around Ellen's legs.

"Wow, that was a lot of potatoes rolling down the mountain. And the angels are taking a lot of pictures. See those flashes!"

Missy peered around her legs. "You said that's not really true."

"No," Ellen admitted. "But it's a good way to think about it."

Ellen closed the door behind them—closed the door to her livelihood and Missy's stability.

Hearing the door open, Ellen glanced over her shoulder. Heather came out. "Ellen, is something wrong?"

Missy detached herself from Ellen's legs and, in the relative quiet, walked over to the racks of newsprint, covered with wet finger paints.

Ellen mouthed the words, not wanting Missy to hear. "Patsy fired me."

"Fi—?" Heather stood with her mouth agape. "Why?"

"Tell you later." She took a deep breath, trying to suppress the mixture of emotions welling up inside, threatening to come forth like a cloudburst. "I'm too religious, so I've just been told."

Heather mouthed, "Ohhh." She raised an eyebrow. "I'll stay awhile and see what Patsy has to say, then I'll come over and you can tell me all about it."

Heather walked back into the classroom.

Missy wailed, holding out a painted finger. "It's still wet."

Ellen took a tissue from her purse and wiped the painted finger, then stuffed the tissue back into her purse. "Your painting will get even more wet and tear up if we take it out in the rain." She took Missy's yellow-and-green rain jacket and matching umbrella off the peg, then reached for her own red one.

She took Missy's papers out of her basket and her extra change of clothes required by the school.

"Come on, we'll have to hurry through the rain. We'll get your painting—" Her words stopped, before she added, "another time."

She'd almost said, "tomorrow."

But there would be no tomorrow here for Ellen.

Nor for Missy.

two

The storm had moved farther away by the time Ellen pulled into the carport beside the long, brick, ranch-style home. She parked behind her dad's car and beside Miss Daisy's. The thunder was now a distant rumble, the lightning infrequent, the wind calmer, and the rain a mere drizzle.

The cloud cover, hanging over the neighborhood as if crying, gave Ellen an even more depressed feeling. Upon exiting the car, she could hear the TV in the living room. Ever since her mom had died, her dad always had it on, as if he couldn't bear the silence of an empty house.

"Take your jacket and shoes off in here, Missy. I'll take care of them in a little bit. Let's see if your clothes are wet."

Ellen slipped out of her own flats, suspecting they were ruined considering the puddles of water she'd waded through. The bottoms of her slacks were wet too. She'd deal with that later.

Ellen could hear Miss Daisy in the next room. "Well, hey, Missy," to which Missy replied, "Hey."

Above the sound of the TV news station, Ellen's dad asked what she was doing home so early.

"On't know," Missy said nonchalantly.

"On't know? What kind of talk is that?"

"On't know," Missy repeated and giggled. Ellen smiled. She'd have to work on Missy's diction, teach her to say clearly, "I don't know."

When she reached the doorway, Ellen's smile broadened as she observed the cozy sight. Her dad and Miss Daisy sat at a card table on which lay a jigsaw puzzle. Maybe Miss Daisy was getting her dad interested in something. He took off his eyeglasses, laid them on the table, and opened his arms to Missy.

13

"I know one thing. Your Pa-Pa needs a hug."

Missy ran over and threw her arms around his chest and made a contented sound as she hugged him tight. He kissed the top of her head. "Hey, you're all wet."

Missy moved back and pointed at his shirt. "You are too."

They both laughed, and he rumpled her already mussed curls.

"Don't they teach you anything at that school?" He tried to sound gruff, but he never fooled Ellen or Missy with the effort. The two of them knew his heart was mush where Missy was concerned.

"I painted a picture. I couldn't bring it 'cause it's still wet."

Ellen remained in the doorway, glorying in the easy camaraderie between that little girl and her Pa-Pa. "You're still wet too. Go to the bathroom." Ellen reminded her.

"Okay. Let me do one piece." She picked up a piece of puzzle and tried to force it into place.

"Missy! Mind your—" Ellen's dad paused and his brow creased.

Had he been about to say, "Mind your Mommy?"

His pause reminded Ellen of Patsy's saying, "That's not true."

He started again. "Mind your manners. Do what Ellen says."

As soon as Missy disappeared down the hallway, Ellen's dad moved his chair back from the card table. "Did the school dismiss early? I wouldn't be surprised if the electricity went off. It flickered here a few times."

Ellen didn't want to worry her dad. And she didn't want to go into details about being fired just yet. It would be common knowledge soon enough. At the moment, she felt the cruel sting of failure. "Dad, I need to talk to you about it."

Miss Daisy stood. "I was just thinking about what to do for supper. But like Jon said, we thought the electricity might go off, so he got out a puzzle."

Ellen saw the blush on Miss Daisy's cheeks. The older woman certainly didn't need to explain her actions to Ellen. If they wanted to bend their gray heads over a puzzle, that was their business. Dad paid Daisy to come in at her convenience and do light cleaning, some shopping, and cook supper on the days she came. Often, they'd have leftovers the following evening, order pizza, or go out. Sometimes on her days off, Daisy would bring over a casserole that she announced was simply too big for her. Ellen suspected Daisy cooked such meals especially for them since she lived alone.

Ellen walked over to the card table. "Looks interesting. Hey, I think this one might fit right there." She picked up a colorful piece to fit into a hot-air balloon. It didn't fit. She laid it back down. "I'm as good at this as Missy."

Even though the three of them laughed lightly, Ellen felt she just didn't fit into this puzzle of a life. She knew to look to the Lord with her problems, but more and more she realized her mom had been such a great source of stability and strength for her and for her dad. Mom had been gone for more than two years. And today was another reminder that things were going from bad to worse.

Daisy put her hand on Ellen's shoulder. Her soft gray eyes held a look of concern that Ellen had seen many times. No, she had not fooled this perceptive woman who was always ready to lend a helping hand. "Honey, let me take care of Missy. I'll get her changed. And I have a new book I brought over for her. I'll read it to her while you talk to your dad."

Ellen acknowledged Daisy's offer to help with a nod. "Thanks."

Watching Daisy proceed down the hallway, Ellen felt a rush of gratitude for her and a stab of regret that her own mom wasn't here to do those things. She turned to her dad, now standing. He nodded toward the kitchen door. "Let's have a cup of coffee."

He picked up the remote and switched off the TV.

❧

Jon Jonsen used to say you could solve your problems over a good cup of coffee. He hadn't said that since Ellen's mom had died. But he did make a mean pot of coffee. That was one thing he didn't even let Daisy do. He didn't like store-bought coffee but preferred the kind that came monthly from a mail-order company. Flavors varied, and he'd spoiled Ellen with their aroma and taste. He was right. The taste was far superior to the supermarket packaged bricks of coffee.

Ellen savored the aroma, put in a dash of creamer, and took a sip. "Mmm, good."

She was ready to tell him the events of the day, but he spoke first. "Daisy was embarrassed."

"Embarrassed?"

He nodded. "Sometimes we sit down and work a puzzle together. Or talk. Or sit and watch a little TV. It's company, you know."

"I think that's great, Dad. You're the one who pays her wages. If you want her to relate to you, that's your business."

He set his cup down. "Not to her way of thinking. She doesn't want to give the wrong impression. She works for me. But we're friends. A few people have asked questions. You know, because she's a widow and I'm without your mom." He took a deep breath, then lifted his cup to his lips. After a swallow of coffee he said emphatically, "We're friends."

Ellen sometimes wondered if Daisy had ideas that went beyond friendship. She was a very nice Christian woman who had worked part-time for her dad for almost two years. Daisy and her husband had attended the same church as Ellen and her parents. Several years ago, Daisy's husband had died after a long illness. Ellen had been a high school student then and simply thought of Daisy as being an older woman. But now that Ellen's own mom had died, she began to have a different view of older people. Her mom was too young to die in her late fifties, and Daisy had just recently passed her sixty-second birthday.

Her dad had wanted someone to come in and help out. "I feel bad enough for your dropping out of college to take care of Missy. But I admire you for it," he'd said. "And your working in a place where you can still be with her all day. I just couldn't bear the thought of her being away from home that long, away from us, after all she's been through."

Now, Ellen had to tell her dad the situation had changed—drastically.

Her dad moved his empty cup aside. He held out his hands, and Ellen placed hers in his, feeling his strength and warmth. His voice held tenderness. "Tell me what's going on, Ellen."

She began. "I was fired."

He listened attentively as she related the episode with Patsy and smiled when she told of her inviting Judy and her mother to church. He nodded with a warm expression in his eyes when she told of singing "Jesus Loves Me" to Missy when the little girl had become frightened of the loud thunder.

When she finished, he squeezed her hands and gazed warmly at her. "I'm proud of you, Ellen."

"But Dad, I should have handled the situation differently. I could have called Judy's mother after work. I could have held Missy, rocked her gently, and hummed the song. She knows the words."

He shook his head. "You instinctively acted on your faith, Ellen. I can't fault you for that."

Ellen withdrew her hands and clasped them on her lap. "I don't know, Dad. It's only a few months until Missy will be in kindergarten. The school has been good for her. And for me. Now—"

She lifted her hands in an idle gesture. "Her life is disrupted again."

"That's not your problem, Ellen."

"Dad." She scoffed. "Of course it's my problem."

When he picked up his empty cup, Ellen thought his hands shook. His voice did not, however. "Maybe this happened for a reason, Ellen. You know I want you to get back in school. Heather's already working on her master's thesis, and you haven't even graduated from college."

"Dad, we've discussed this before. Missy's more important than college. A few months can be like a lifetime to a child."

With that unrelenting look on his face, he got up and

headed for the coffee pot.

She turned in her chair, watching him pour. "I need to get a job, maybe with another day-care facility for the summer. Missy needs me with her."

He stood gazing out the window over the sink, holding onto the cup with both hands as if it might get away. "You don't need a job, Ellen. You've taken on too much responsibility already. Take the summer off. Get ready to return to college in the fall. This could very well be God's closing a door so you can walk through another one."

At the moment, Ellen's faith wasn't quite strong enough to take comfort in that comment. "Dad, I could register for college in the fall. But I still need to be with Missy this summer."

He set his cup down, turned his back on her momentarily, and held onto the countertop. Ellen wondered at the rise of his shoulders. Was he not taking her being fired as calmly as he'd seemed? Had he just said those things to help her feel better? Was he worried about Missy?

"Dad?"

He turned, facing her. His body looked stiff. His words were abrupt. "Get on with your life, Ellen. You're not her mother. Which reminds me. There's a note from Leanne in the mail."

Leanne—Missy's birth mother. Ellen sucked in her breath. She'd thought the storm was over, but she felt it churning in the pit of her stomach, and it seemed a cloudburst exploded in her chest. What had happened to that warmth and his sense of being proud of her?

His coffee untouched and his chin set in a stubborn way, her dad strode from the kitchen without looking at her.

His words echoed in her mind repeatedly: *You are not Missy's mother.*

Ellen wanted release from the storm inside her. But the confusion and hurt simply deepened as her world turned darker. The storm did not subside, nor did it allow release in the form of tears. She pushed it back and let it lie alongside her dream that her mother had not died. She wished she had not been fired and caused this additional burden on her dad and on Missy.

Ellen knew she'd be all right after the shock of being fired wore off. She'd talk to her dad at a more convenient time and try to get to the bottom of what he meant. If she was doing something wrong, she wanted to know.

Her gaze focused on the stack of mail and found the letter from Leanne. With a heavy heart, she pulled out a lovely card with flowers on the front and imprinted in big letters, "Thinking of You."

> *Dear Uncle Jon and Ellen,*
> *Hope everyone is well. I'm great! I just got a bit part in a soap opera. That could lead to all sorts of things.*
> *Give sweet Missy a big hug and kiss for me.*
>
> *Love,*
> *Leanne*
>
> *P.S. I'm Carla Coatsworth in the soap* Love's Sweet Promise. *I'll let you know when it airs.*

The salutation was almost longer than the message!

Ellen reprimanded herself immediately for feeling sarcastic. Maybe she was just jealous. Leanne had a job. Only nineteen years old, Leanne had broken into acting, something she'd wanted to do since childhood. Winning a local, then state, beauty contest had made a difference. She was a beautiful blond with blue eyes. Missy was the spitting image of her.

Ellen shivered. Leanne was not Carla. That was only a role she played. And three times today—first by Patsy, then her dad, and now Leanne—Ellen had been reminded that she was not Missy's mom. Ellen's mom and dad had adopted Missy, but Ellen had been like a mother to the child for the past two years. Did everyone else feel that Ellen was not Missy's mommy? That it was only a role she played?

three

"I'll fix supper tonight," Ellen said when Daisy and Jon walked into the kitchen.

"I'll just go on then," Daisy replied. "The way that rain came down, I might have water coming in under the garage door."

"If you have water in your basement, call me, Daisy," Ellen's dad insisted. "I'll come over and help bail it out."

"That only happens about once a year, Jon, when so much rain falls so fast."

"Well, you let me know," he said. "And Daisy, Ellen losing her job doesn't affect yours in any way."

Ellen wondered what exactly was going on. She'd tried to be considerate by telling Daisy she could leave. Had her dad wanted Daisy to stay and cook supper?

Daisy turned to her and smiled sweetly. "Don't worry about your job, Honey. Remember, tests can become testimonies. I should know. I've been through enough of them."

Ellen nodded, returning the smile.

Daisy took her leave, and Ellen closed the back door behind her, wondering if she could ever be a walking testimony like Daisy was. She felt more like a false witness. Instead of gaining in maturity, she was obviously inept at everything she tried to do.

Neither Ellen nor her dad spoke as they heard Daisy's car leaving the driveway. Ellen turned to face him, wondering if she should try to communicate better. His comments about her job loss made her sense of failure that much greater.

The sound of knocking at the back door and the sudden pressure of the door being pushed against her back interrupted her thoughts. She hastily stepped back from the door.

Heather's face, surrounded by wheat-colored hair, peeked

around the edge of the door. "Hey, what kind of welcome is this? You could at least use the deadlock instead of your body. I'm stronger than you, Girl."

Ellen was grateful for Heather's bubbly personality that had a way of bringing out positive responses in people. Dad laughed along with Ellen and invited Heather in out of the weather.

Missy ran into the kitchen just then, waving a video of *The Lion King*. She looked at Ellen. "You promised."

Ellen's dad put his hand on Missy's shoulder. "Don't you think you should speak to Heather?"

Missy looked at Heather, then up at the older man. "No. I spoke to her all day long."

He laughed. "Okay. I guess you have a point there." He lifted a little blond ringlet and let it fall back in place. "Let's you and me go watch *The Lion King* while these girls whip us up one fine supper."

Heather plopped down in a chair. "If that's an invitation, I accept, Mr. Jonsen."

Missy huffed and put her free hand on her hip. "He's not Mr. Jonsen. He's Pa-Pa."

With the heel of her hand, Heather pushed against her own forehead. "Oops. Sorry, Pa-Pa."

Missy ran on into the living room with the video.

Ellen's dad looked at the two friends. "I can hardly wait. I've only seen it two dozen times."

Heather laughed with him. "You're a good Pa-Pa."

He pushed his glasses further up on his nose. "Well, I hedge a little. I tell Missy I like to read the paper or a magazine while I watch TV. Never limit yourself to one thing."

"She lets you get by with that?"

"For the most part. She only tells me every minute or so that the good part's coming on, and I've just gotta watch." He headed for the living room.

"You're gonna cook, huh?" Heather questioned.

Ellen tried to make a joke of it. "This might be our last

full-course meal for awhile, now that I'm out of work."

Her dad turned back and took a few steps toward Ellen and Heather. "Now, Ellen, don't go saying things like that. Some people might believe it, and you know little pitchers have big ears."

"I'll set her straight, Dad. I was joking."

"And understand this," he continued, "we don't have to worry about money, and you don't have to worry about a job, Ellen. What's mine is yours and that little girl's."

Ellen nodded. She spoke weakly. "Thanks, Dad."

After he left the room, Ellen shook her head and sighed. "I don't know what's wrong with him. . .or me."

Heather ignored the comment. A long lock of hair fell along her face. She pushed it behind her ear. "Where did that saying come from? Little pitchers have big ears?"

Ellen shrugged. "I don't know. Mom used to say it, and so did Grandma. I guess they used to have little pitchers. Maybe they called the handles 'ears.' "

Heather grinned. "Sounds more like a Little League baseball player to me."

"Does, doesn't it? Anyway, let me elaborate on what Dad said before you start thinking about working up a care package for us. Mom's insurance left plenty of money; and even the house is paid for."

Heather nodded. "That's a blessing."

"But it's not mine, Heather. It's Dad's. I've got to make my own way."

"You're doing more than that, Ellen, the way you take care of Missy."

"Oh, yeah! The way I take care of her is to lose my job, alienate my dad, appear to take over Daisy's job—"

"Oh, quit feeling sorry for yourself. Tell me what happened."

Is that what I'm doing? Feeling sorry for myself? I don't think so. It's all about Missy. But I need to quit dwelling on it and go forward. But where? And how?

Ellen walked over to the refrigerator, took out a package of frozen ground beef, and set it on the countertop near the microwave, getting ready to thaw it out. Suddenly, she looked at Heather. "Hey. This is supposed to be a joint effort. We're having Missy's favorite meal—spaghetti." She pointed to the refrigerator. "Dad said you and I were fixing supper. There's lettuce in there just waiting to be torn, tomatoes to dice, eggs to—"

Heather stood and gave a mock grumble. "Thought you'd never ask."

While they prepared the meal, Ellen told Heather what had transpired with Patsy.

Heather rinsed her hands after dicing tomatoes and wiped them on a paper towel. "There's got to be more to it, Ellen. You and I talked about things happening at church, and so you sang 'Jesus Loves Me' to Missy. That's not enough to be fired over. There's something wrong with Patsy."

Ellen gazed at Heather. "Everybody knows Patsy is perfect."

Heather nodded. "She's good at what she does, all right. And that's an important part of my thesis. But something's eating at her. Maybe she's under some kind of religious conviction."

"Yeah. Convicted that I'm not to work there anymore." Ellen sighed. "But even if that were true, Heather. She got rid of me. So there goes my witness—if I ever was one."

Heather lifted her finger. "Ah, ha! But I'm there. She can't fire me because she didn't hire me. She wants the publicity I can give Little Tykes. She wants to win that award for the best preschool in the nation."

The buzzer sounded, and Ellen turned off the heat from under the boiled eggs. "Well, do what you must. In the meantime, I have to do something about preschool for Missy and getting a job."

"A lot of children take the summers off from school and make it just fine. Missy probably wouldn't mind that. Your dad seems to take good care of her, and you can tell he loves her." She smiled. "He's a good man."

Ellen agreed. They didn't come any better. "But something's wrong with him, Heather. I think he just can't get over Mom's dying. He looks at Missy sometimes with sadness in his eyes and gets a distant look on his face. His mind is off somewhere on something else instead of on us, and when I get his attention, I have to repeat what I said."

"You don't think it might be anything serious, do you? Like. . .Alzheimer's?"

"No. It's not like he can't concentrate or can't remember. It's more like he just has something else on his mind. So, you see, I think Missy is better off at a day-care facility. But I don't know if she'd be happy there without me."

Heather sighed and shook her head. "Let me think."

She thought for a matter of about two seconds. "I know the perfect place. I'm including Ridgeway Conference Center's preschool in my thesis."

Ellen knew Heather's project involved comparing and reporting on various kinds of schools. "I didn't know they had a preschool."

"Oh yeah. And summer programs too, for children. And day care for conferees' children. I worked there a couple of summers. Remember?"

"You worked at the girls' camp, didn't you?"

"Yeah. But I know about all the other programs. They didn't have a preschool then, but they do now."

"One major drawback," Ellen said. "I can't give Patsy as a reference."

"Why not?" Heather looked determined. "Being fired for proselytizing should work in your favor at Ridgeway."

Ellen sighed. "I doubt Patsy would say that."

Heather nodded. "You're probably right. But that would impress the personnel manager, if he's the same one who hired me."

"Who's that?"

"Richard Williams. He was a neat guy." Heather looked as if she'd landed on the perfect solution to Ellen's dilemma. "So I'll be your reference. I've observed you at work. When I get through singing your praises, they'll probably make you director of that conference center." She frowned. "Well, not the director just yet. He's the one who gave permission for me to report on their preschool."

They both laughed. Ellen could always count on Heather as a blessing. She just might be a good reference since she'd worked at Ridgeway, had permission to report on their preschool, and was a Christian. Her commendation of Ellen's qualifications might mean more to Ridgeway than Patsy's assessment. She could also use her pastor as a reference and maybe Daisy.

"And too," Heather said, "instead of watching *The Lion King,* Missy would learn about the King of kings."

That settled the matter for Ellen. "I'll call now. You know the telephone number of Ridgeway?"

Heather shook her head. "Don't remember. Where's your phone book?"

Within the next couple of minutes, Ellen was on the phone asking about getting an application. She hung up, smiling. "You want to thaw out this hamburger and start the spaghetti sauce while I run up there?"

"I know it's only a couple of miles away, El, but I'd suggest you drive."

"Ah," Ellen jested, "I knew I kept you around for something."

❧

"Not another one, MaryJo," Richard Williams groaned when his administrative assistant came into his office and slipped another application beneath the stack next to the folder he'd been perusing.

"It just came up from the front desk. But no more today, I promise."

He glanced over at her. "Don't make promises you can't keep. That baby can hear you, you know."

"Would I lie to my baby?" With a triumphant grin, she laid her hands on her stomach. "My doctor's appointment, remember? I'm leaving early."

He leaned back, releasing some of the tension in his

shoulders from having bent over the application folders for most of the afternoon.

MaryJo placed her hand on a couple of folders at the corner of the desk. "These two cancelled because of the storm."

"Makes you wonder if they'd show up for work in a storm, doesn't it?" Richard said with a shake of his head.

MaryJo agreed. "This one—Ellen Jonsen—is either a duck, or eager for a job, to have come out in weather like this."

Richard agreed, then glanced over his shoulder to the windows behind him. "Looks like the worst is over. But you be careful out there."

MaryJo sighed and looked toward the ceiling. She spoke in monotone. "Yes, Sir. I'll drive home and have Ben drive me to the doctor. So, with a man in the driver's seat, I feel confident we'll be just fine."

Richard nodded. "That eases my mind some. He's the driver and you're the copilot. You're pretty good at telling men how to do their jobs."

"Is that a compliment?"

Richard pointed at himself and grimaced. "Would I do that?"

"Not often." She shook her head, but her eyes held warmth and her lips smiled.

He waved her off. "Hope all goes well."

She grew as serious as he. "Thanks."

His glance swept over her retreating form before he swivelled his chair toward the windows being pattered by the diminishing rain. He hardly noticed the rain. His thoughts were with MaryJo, Ben, and the baby due to make its appearance before long.

He'd appreciated MaryJo since she came to work for him five years ago, right out of secretarial school. He'd observed her grow up. Her plans changed; her conversations changed from movies she saw to where she and Ben went and where she and Ben would go on vacation. For months now, the conversation had been dominated by descriptions of how they were turning a bedroom into a nursery, surprise baby showers, doctor's appointments, and baby clothes. He'd learned that a certain kind of yelp from her office meant the baby had kicked again.

Richard rejoiced that a young couple was so in love and so obviously thrilled about starting a family. When Ben came around, he still talked about sports or movies, but he never failed to mention the baby.

As director of human resources, Richard had many opportunities to watch young people return to Ridgeway summer after summer and grow in work experience and faith. He believed that God, in His great mercy, had placed him in a position where he played a part, even if indirectly, in their spiritual growth.

He knew firsthand about irresponsible behavior that could irrevocably change the course of a person's life. Having gone to church all his life, he'd known right from wrong and as a child had even claimed Jesus as his Savior. Yet, he'd sinned. The consequences of his sin had resulted in his falling on his face, so to speak. Thankfully, he'd known where to turn for help and had fallen on his knees in repentance and committed his life to Christian service.

Some people spoke openly about their past sins and used that as a wonderful testimony to God's forgiveness and grace. Richard had never felt the need to do that, choosing instead to witness to his Christian faith by the way he now lived his life.

Suddenly, he slapped the arms of his chair. *Why am I sitting here, doing nothing?*

The weather—that was it. Dreary days had a way of seeping into his skin, getting under it.

He swivelled back to the desk and started to pick up the top folder. His fingers drummed against it, as if he had to allow one more pressing thought before returning to work.

He sighed. His position allowed him to see changes and growth in staff and conferees, but his own life was pretty much constant. And until now, that had been just the way he liked it.

four

Friday morning, before nine o'clock, Ellen drove with Missy along the road that wound up and around Ridgeway's registration building. It loomed white and gleaming, four stories high. The blue sky was brushed with only a few white streaks of thin, washed-out clouds. The air smelled fresh, and everything looked clean from yesterday's drenching. Puddles of water still lay in holes and ditches. The ground remained soggy.

Ellen looked up on the mountainside to where work trucks were parked in front of a new hotel being built. The several-story structure dwarfed the small preschool below it. She parked in one of the spaces marked off at the side of the road. Parents with small children were exiting their cars. Bigger children ran from their cars over to the bridge. Some cars were leaving, others pulling in.

Ellen saw no cartoon characters, just a small sign identifying the building that looked like an adorable, storybook cottage. Missy had her door open and ran to the wooden bridge spanning the rushing waters of the swollen creek that ran alongside the road. She joined other children exclaiming, "Look. Baby ducks."

"Be careful now," Ellen called. "Don't lean over too far."

Missy put her arms on top of the wooden railing. She stood on tiptoes, peering over the railing at little speckled ducks following their mother down the creek and under the bridge. Ellen observed that the mother had her ducks in a row—something she couldn't say for herself.

Missy ran to the other side of the bridge to see them emerge. "Can I pet them?"

"They're moving too fast for that. Maybe later we can go to the lake and feed the ducks. I'll bet there are a lot of little ones there. But right now, let's see what this school is like. Okay?"

"Okay." Missy walked along with her as a couple of women smiled and spoke, while other parents tried to pry their children away from the bridge.

Ellen hung back with Missy on the porch that stretched across the front of the cottage and was surrounded by a white wooden banister. After the others went in, Ellen followed with Missy in hand. They stood in the foyer.

Smiling women with warmth in their eyes greeted the children, who rushed past them toward the play items designed to inspire eagerness for education. Most of the students gathered around a cage containing a calico cat. Others rushed to a huge plastic Noah's Ark and began matching animals, two by two, and placing them in the ark.

Yesterday, after handing in her application, Ellen had asked about the preschool and been given the name of the director, whom she called later in the evening. The director, Carol Freeman, invited Ellen and Missy to come and look it over.

After the children were in their rooms and the other parents had left, a woman held out her hand. "You must be Ellen," to which Ellen responded affirmatively. "And this is Missy."

The petite woman with a pleasant face surrounded by short curly hair smiled at Ellen, then devoted her attention to Missy. She knelt in front of Missy, who still held onto Ellen's hand. "Missy, I'm so glad you came to see us this morning. Would you like to take a look at Callie while I talk to your mommy?"

Mommy. While half-listening to Carol, Ellen realized that when she'd talked to the director on the phone, she'd said "I have a four-year-old, almost five. . . ," and Carol had assumed Missy was her child.

Carol was explaining that Callie was her cat that she brought to class every day and let spend some time in the classroom, although she played outside much of the time. "Could you do that while I talk with your mom?"

Missy nodded.

Carol must have caught the gleam in Missy's eyes. "Just don't put your fingers inside the cage. Callie likes to play and paw at the children, but she doesn't realize how sharp her claws are." Carol stood and called to a worker sitting at a small table, watching the children. "Jan, Missy would like to see Callie. Would you have her join in the activities while I talk to her mom?"

"Sure," Jan said, lightly touching Missy's back. "I have some other very interesting things to show you. Would you believe we can make it rain on Noah's ark?"

Missy snickered and looked up at Jan with excited eyes, her blond curls bouncing against her face as she shook her head.

Carol laughed. "The rain comes at the end of the day. The children love it. Serves a double purpose. We spray a little disinfectant soap on the ark and figures. It helps with keeping the plastic figures clean." Carol looked at Missy, who seemed eager to join the other children. "She'll be fine."

Ellen nodded and walked with Carol down a hallway and into a small office. There was barely room for the desk and an extra chair. Different from Patsy's big office. The room Missy had gone into was different too. It looked like many children's Sunday school classrooms, with pictures depicting Bible stories, including Jesus with little children at His knees and on His lap.

Ellen told Carol about being fired and the reason for the action.

"Little Tykes is reportedly one of the best in teaching children," Carol admitted. "Patsy Hatcher is known for being tops when it comes to running a preschool." Carol sighed. "But here, we stress the love of Jesus and how He wants us to live."

Ellen nodded. "Missy gets that at home and at church, but it would be wonderful if she could be here, where that is stressed as well. One can never get too much of a good thing."

Carol returned her smile. "Right. That can be said for most of us, I'm sure."

"Could you take Missy?"

Carol sat thoughtful for a moment, then looked across at Ellen. "You're in luck. Ooops, sorry. I forgot. Christians don't have luck. We have blessings." She grinned. "You're blessed. We had a cancellation at the first of the week, due to a family situation. The families on our waiting list had already placed their children elsewhere." She looked toward the door for a moment, then back at Ellen. "I don't see any reason why Missy wouldn't fit right in. But of course, when there are situations of not relating well, we deal with that."

"Missy's not shy."

Carol smiled. "I didn't think so. Oh, you need to know. Preschool dismisses at two. Then day-care workers come and stay with Ridgeway employees' children and a few other students until their parents get off work. All children must be picked up by five."

At least she had a place for Missy—in a Christian environment. But what about herself? Ellen took a deep breath, then plunged in. "Since I was fired, I'm looking for a job. Do you have any openings?"

A slow shake of Carol's head indicated to Ellen there were none.

"Your having worked at Little Tykes for almost two years speaks well of your abilities," Carol said, "as does the reason you were fired in relation to what we expect of our workers. We are to be vocal about Jesus and stress Christian principles."

Ellen needed some kind of confirmation of being worthwhile. Although she didn't feel she'd done anything that she deserved to be fired for, there was still the stigma of being fired from a job where you were responsible for children. Any secular day-care director would likely feel the same way as Patsy. And too, she'd felt Patsy was her friend. That was just another loss, piled onto the others.

"I wish I could hire you," Carol said, "but the same workers have been here for several years, and there's a waiting list for workers too." She shrugged a shoulder. "I don't know of anyone planning to leave, and although we could never have too many workers, I doubt that the personnel manager is hiring additional ones. We have a limit both on the number of children and of workers."

Ellen tried not to show her disappointment.

"Won't hurt to try, though," Carol said. "But I'm not the one who does the hiring. The director of human resources does get my approval and have me interview prospective workers."

Ellen understood. "I filled out an application yesterday."

Carol smiled. "I can show you around so you can see what all we do. You'll need to fill out some forms for Missy. I'm sure Little Tykes required medical records."

Ellen nodded. "They require a life-history of the children and the parents."

"Not a bad idea," Carol said. "If you'd like to leave Missy today, that would be fine, since she's been accustomed to being in school. Your little girl's a beauty."

My little girl. "Oh, I almost forgot. I guess I need to tell you this. Missy calls me Mommy. But she isn't my daughter."

Carol listened as Ellen related the relationship and the situation. "My parents adopted Missy. After Mom died two years ago, I've filled the role of mother. Missy calls me 'Mommy,' and I've allowed it. I'm her mom in every way except legally. Officially, she's my little sister."

When she finished, Carol stood and reached out her hand. "Ellen, I'm more impressed with you now than when you came in."

The compliment meant a lot to Ellen. But Patsy, then Ellen's dad, had reminded her she wasn't Missy's mom. Now Ellen had to admit it to Carol.

She had a sinking feeling. Was God forcing her to admit it to herself?

જ

Richard looked up and stretched his shoulders when MaryJo came into the office with a scrap of paper. "Carol, at the day care, sent a note to go in one of the files. She was impressed with this applicant."

"Okay, which one?"

"I put it at the bottom of the pile." MaryJo lifted the others. "Yes, here it is. Ellen Jonsen." She held it out.

Richard opened the folder and slipped the note inside. He appreciated additional background information on a prospective employee and valued others' opinions.

He scanned the information. Ellen Jonsen. Not a college student. Twenty-four years old. Had experience in a well-respected preschool.

Her name didn't ring a bell, but the reference person did: Heather Cannington.

"Somebody mentioned her at lunch the other day," Richard said. "Something about her writing an article on the preschool."

"Oh, is she the one? Martha mentioned that, but she didn't know who was doing the article. So, it's Heather."

"You know her?"

"Not really." MaryJo laughed. "Remember the incident with Jeff Blount a few years ago?"

"Right." No wonder that name had sounded so familiar. Richard began to nod. It was all coming back. He grinned. "They both denied anything serious between them."

MaryJo smiled. "You gave them the benefit of the doubt. So maybe that was true. As far as I recall, there was never any other problem with them."

"Right. And the next year Jeff came back, but she didn't."

MaryJo nodded. "She still has her maiden name." She reached for the file.

Richard held it out, then drew it back toward himself. "Just leave it on the desk. I'll take another look at it later on." In his quick scan, he'd noted that the applicant had indicated interest in day-care or children's programs and a willingness to work full time, part-time, permanent, or temporary. She'd consider any job. Sounded rather desperate, like she'd take anything.

There wasn't a "desperate" tab on any of the folders. However, that's how his mind registered a few applicants whose information crossed his desk. He'd much prefer thinking about the college students who likely would take a no with a grain of salt and think it was his loss by not hiring them. But the desperate ones touched his heart. Those were the ones he'd really like to help. But usually, he had to send word that he couldn't use them. He didn't say they lacked required skills but that usually was the reason.

Several times, he made notes on applications for MaryJo to deal with. "Can't use this one. This one is too young for the summer program this year, will consider for next summer. Have this one come in to talk to me. This one is a possibility for the new hotel."

He kept thinking about the "desperate" folder. The applicant wrote that her job at Little Tykes ended on Thursday. Apparently, she'd come directly to apply at Ridgeway. She'd come in the flooded streets when two other applicants had cancelled their interviews because of the storm.

Impressive.

He wouldn't need workers for several weeks for the new hotel. He could interview her, discover if he should keep the application on file for future reference and also determine if she was a candidate for hotel registration clerk, housekeeping, or the dining room.

He hoped he would never see prospective applicants as just names on paper. They were human beings trying to find their place in the world. As director of human resources, his responsibilities included helping them do just that.

His glance moved to the corner of his desk.

Ten minutes before MaryJo would leave for the day, he rang her office. "MaryJo, make an appointment for Ellen Johnson to come in for an interview toward the end of next week, please."

five

Things were looking up.

And happening quickly.

The day after being fired from Little Tykes, Ellen had Missy enrolled in another preschool. This one was located in a Christian environment, no less.

Then late that same afternoon, Mr. Williams's administrative assistant had called, asking if she could come in for an interview the following Thursday afternoon at four o'clock.

Could she ever!

All week, Ellen couldn't help but feel positive about the situation.

But when Thursday arrived, she wasn't sure how to dress for the interview. Slacks had been fine for Little Tykes, considering one could expect the inevitable stains from fingerprints of myriad consistencies and textures, splashed finger paints, and grass or mud stains. She'd begun to wear her hair in an easy, simple ponytail. For the interview, she decided to let it fall in soft waves to her shoulders. The days of spring sunshine had already begun to bring out the golden highlights in her light brown hair.

She would look feminine, but conservative. She chose a pastel yellow sleeveless dress with a matching short-sleeved jacket. Two-inch heels instead of flats, small gold earrings, and a little more care with her makeup completed the transformation, although she preferred a more natural look. The few freckles across the bridge of her nose had long been an accepted part of her appearance, and she no longer tried to hide them as she had in high school days.

She looked herself over in a full-length mirror and felt pleased. Suddenly, she had an eerie thought. Suppose the personnel manager wanted to hire her full time? Would she still want to stay on after the summer, even after Missy started kindergarten?

Maybe she should work in the summer program instead of day care. That way she'd be free to go on to college or get a job. This was an issue she could talk about with Mr. Williams.

"Oh, you look so pretty," Daisy said when Ellen walked into the kitchen. The widow was putting the final touches on a casserole she was about to pop into the oven.

Ellen's dad sat at the table, munching on Daisy's famous molasses cookies and reading a fishing magazine. He looked Ellen over, then sighed as he laid the magazine on the table with a little more force than necessary. He spoke the same way. "You should be looking like a college girl, Ellen. Not somebody off to take some highfalutin job."

"Dad." Ellen felt like he'd let the air out of her confidence balloon. "We've been though this a dozen times, just in the past week."

He frowned. "You don't seem to be listening to me."

"Yes, I do. But I'm a grown woman. I have to start making my own way."

"You're not supposed to be a grown woman. You're a college-aged kid."

Fighting the emotion his comments evoked, she looked at her watch. "I have to go."

She stole a look at Daisy, who gave her a sweet, sympathetic look. The older woman mouthed, "You're okay," and smiled.

Ellen tried to get back into her good mood, but her dad had a way of spoiling it. Whatever had happened to that good-natured man who used to be her dad?

He'd said more than once that when Ellen's mom died two years ago, something had died inside him. Maybe he was right.

All Ellen knew was that she just couldn't do anything to please him anymore. And at a time when she needed him most, since her mom was no longer here, he remained distant.

Moments later, Ellen walked through one of the many glass

doors at the front of the conference registration building. She turned to her left and ascended the curved stairs. At the top, she stepped onto the carpet of a long room surrounded by a wrought-iron railing. She looked down upon the lobby, decorated with cozy-looking furniture surrounded by potted plants and small trees. The tall glass windows, two stories high, revealed a spectacular display of mountainsides, coming alive with the look of spring.

Remembering the assistant's directions, she walked to her left again, pushed open one of the double doors, and made her way down a long hallway to an open door labeled "Richard Williams, Director of Human Resources."

Ellen stood for a moment and breathed a silent prayer for this interview to go well. This was Missy's fifth day at the preschool. She loved the activities and the teachers more each day. When Ellen had questioned her, she'd said she missed her old friends but had made new ones. She was eager to go each morning and see the cat and ducks. She'd begun to beg for a kitten of her own.

In a way, Ellen regretted not having thought of Ridgeway's preschool or day care in the first place.

Another failing of hers?

But then, it had worked well, her and Missy being at Little Tykes together. That had perhaps been best. She had thought it God's will. If so, was it now God's will that she be fired? Confusion rang dominant in her mind. She must put aside the idea of failure and walk into that office with confidence. Otherwise, she'd never be hired.

"Come on in," a female voice called.

Ellen realized she had been staring at the maroon carpet in the hallway. She looked ahead at a very pregnant woman who waddled across the floor, opened a file drawer, and slipped a folder into it. "I'm Ellen Jonsen."

"Hi. I'm MaryJo." She patted her protruding abdomen. "And this is Tyler. I can tell he's going to be a professional football kicker."

Ellen laughed with her. "Nice to meet. . .both of you."

MaryJo's outgoing manner and animated face put Ellen at ease. She sat in a chair that the assistant indicated. "Mr. Williams is kind of a stickler about time. At four, I'll let him know you're here."

Ellen glanced at the clock on the wall. Seven minutes to wait. At least she wasn't late for this "stickler about time."

Ellen needn't have worried about time crawling, however. After MaryJo questioned whether she'd ever be able to walk across a room again without waddling from side-to-side, she began talking about her baby. She slowly lowered herself into the leather chair behind her desk and expelled a deep breath as if sitting down had been quite a chore. After that, Ellen learned all about baby Tyler.

&

Richard Williams closed the "desperate" file after making notes about his impression of the applicant. Several items raised warning flags. But that's why a person in his position was needed—to weed through such things.

The wall clock indicated he had five minutes before the scheduled appointment. He expected punctuality but felt no need to give the impression he wanted employees on the job early. He could hear voices in the outer office, but a five minute wait would be best.

He turned the swivel chair to face the windows that revealed the panoramic view of mountainsides, lushly green. A week had passed since the big storm in the area. All looked bright on the horizon.

A sudden sense of restlessness assaulted him. It happened occasionally. Even a line of poetry trotted through his brain: *Spring is when a young man's fancy turns to love.* With a mental shake of his head and a wry grin, he reminded himself he wasn't a spring chicken anymore, at age thirty-four. And he'd redefined the definition of love eons ago.

Besides, spring was nearing its end. The rains, storms, and wind had subsided, bringing in the long-anticipated May flowers that would be followed by June's mild temperatures and the busy schedule at the conference center. Summer was knocking at the door.

Like a knock on his consciousness, his intercom sounded. "Mr. Williams. Your four o'clock appointment is here."

Richard turned toward the desk. "Send her in, please."

He touched the knot on his tie, although knowing it was still in place. It had nowhere else to go. That taken care of, he cleared his throat and was ready to stand when the hesitant applicant would enter as if she held the key to her future.

Richard felt first impressions were important. His brought surprise. In no way did this applicant appear desperate. Ellen Jonsen made a favorable impression as far as looks were concerned. The overall picture was of an attractive young woman, conservatively dressed, nice, nothing to detract, positively or negatively. He'd say. . .average. She looked to be in her mid-twenties, as typed on the application form.

He stood. "Miss Jonsen."

She nodded.

He reached his hand across his desk. "I'm Richard Williams." They shook hands. "Please be seated."

She sat opposite him in one of the brown leather chairs with arms.

Upon closer look, he realized she wasn't exactly average. He watched as she pushed her light brown hair away from her face. She was quite pretty. Her eyes seemed to be a soft brown with a hint of gold, perhaps reflecting the sunlight shining outside the windows behind him.

She lowered her hand and grasped her purse as if someone might snatch it. That spoke of uncertainty. She looked across at him with concern in her eyes.

He wanted to set her mind at ease. She was certainly qualified to work in the preschool, day-care center, or in the children's summer programs.

But her reference was a coworker, not the director. He opened the folder in front of him. "I see your reference is

Heather Cannington." He looked across at her. "A few years back, a young woman by that name worked here a couple of summers with the girl's camp."

"Yes, she did. Between high school and college, then after her first year of college."

"And she's working at Little Tykes now?"

"No, she's working on her master's thesis in child development and goes to the school quite often, doing research. She helps out too. Several times a week, for several months, she's observed my work."

Richard leaned back against his chair. "So Miss Cannington is going into child development?"

"No. She wants to write children's books. She thought a minor in English lit and a major in child development would give her a good background."

"Mmmm. Impressive."

"So you. . .do remember her?" Miss Jonsen asked tentatively.

Richard laughed lightly. "Oh, I remember—" He stopped and covered what he was about to say with a clearing of his throat. Some things were confidential. And what he remembered had happened several years ago. "She was. . .interesting." He forced the smile from his face and turned his attention to the application.

This interview was not about Heather Cannington but about Miss Jonsen. And two questions loomed large in his mind. Why was she changing jobs, since this one paid no more than she had been making? And why was her letter of reference from a student doing research for her master's degree instead of from a coworker or the director?

The brief turn of her lips upward when he'd smiled at her indicated to him she wasn't really in a smiling mood.

He clasped his hands together, then rested them on top of her application. No need to rehash the obvious. She was twenty-four and had majored in communications at the area university.

"You didn't graduate from college?"

"No, I left midway through my senior year. Are you only considering college graduates?"

Richard felt on the defensive for a moment. "No, no. We have some summer employees who are just entering college in the fall. I was just curious."

She nodded but offered no explanation. He realized the issue was really none of his business. He leaned back against his leather swivel chair and let his hands rest on his pants legs. "Tell me, Miss Jonsen. If you were to leave this world and could come back as an animal, what animal would it be?"

Her eyes widened. Very expressive eyes. Sort of golden brown. Hazel, he supposed.

"Is this a quiz or something to see what I'd say to children about, um, animals?"

Apparently, she wasn't into playing games today. Except, this wasn't a game. He took it seriously. "No game. It's something I ask most applicants. How about playing along?" He'd just said it wasn't a game, yet he'd asked her to play along. What was happening to his professionalism? Just because it wasn't everyday such an attractive, appealing woman walked into his office. And he shouldn't be thinking that way. That's the last thing he needed. . .or wanted. "That's a question I ask those I feel are qualified for a position."

She stared. "Well, I really expect to go to heaven when I die, and I don't believe in reincarnation."

"I understand that. This is a make-believe situation. Just a fun question. Do you mind answering it?"

Suppose she refused? Would he ask her to leave? One thing was for sure—she didn't just go along with something because you asked. She weighed the pros and cons. That was good. Wasn't it?

"I suppose. . ." She spoke up just as he was about to change the subject. "I suppose I'd come back as a bird."

"Bird?"

"Not just any old bird. Like a vulture or anything." She sounded a little self-conscious. "Maybe. . .a finch. No, a canary. Yes." Her eyes brightened. "A canary."

"Why a canary?"

"They're pretty. Yellow."

You're far from yellow—well, her outfit was—but you are pretty. Trying to rein in his straying thoughts, he smiled and nodded at her, saying nothing.

"They fly." She waved her hand. "Just take off into the clear blue sky. That must be a wonderfully free feeling."

Ah, she wanted to be free. Of what? Of whom?

"Oh, and they sing. I don't have a great voice, but I'd love to just sing away as I suspect a canary does. Yes. I'd have to be a singing canary."

She seemed relaxed now. They were in sync. Asking the animal question generally put an applicant at ease. There was always a certain amount of tension, no matter how confident the applicant, since the final outcome rested with him.

"Oh, and I think it would be great to find pieces of colored Easter grass to weave into a nest. Then sit on little tiny eggs and sing until they hatch. And it would be fun being the early bird that gets the worm." She paused. "If. . .I were a canary."

Yes, the nesting instinct. Rearing children seemed to be most women's natural desire. Men's too, for that matter.

His intent had been to have her reveal something about her inner character and not just say something she thought a prospective employer wanted to hear.

"Mr. Williams," she said, "what animal would you be?"

six

Her question rendered Richard speechless for a moment. An applicant had never asked that during an interview. After he'd hired Jerry and they'd become friends, Jerry had asked. They'd discussed it and laughed about what kind of animal each might be.

Kidding, Richard had replied, "A louse," before answering Jerry's question seriously.

He believed Miss Jonsen was serious. Come to think about it, she had as much right to know the inner characteristics of people she might work with as those who did the hiring. He answered, "I think I'd be a lion." He raised his hand in a cautionary gesture. "Don't get me wrong. I don't roar a lot."

She laughed lightly, then smiled. A cute dimple punctuated her right cheek. "Why a lion?"

"Protective of my territory, I've been told." He looked at his wristwatch although the clock across from him was clearly visible. "Afraid we'll have to bypass delving into that."

He hoped he'd given the impression there wasn't time to answer. Although he had an inclination toward conversation with Miss Jonsen, he reminded himself of the purpose of their encounter. He looked at the application, although he knew its contents.

When he glanced up again, he asked, "Why did you leave your job, Miss Jonsen?"

Her dimple disappeared. "I was fired."

Her response caught him as off guard as her charisma had. "Fired?"

She nodded. "While on the property, I invited one of the mothers to my church after her child had expressed interest in one of the church's programs. And I openly talked with

43

another person about our mutual faith. Heather, to be exact. I didn't proselytize. We just enjoyed talking about the church, a faith question. It was as natural to me as talking about seeing a certain movie or TV program. I tried, but I can't pretend that God isn't a vital part of my life."

He listened intently as Miss Jonsen related the reasons behind her dismissal. His admiration and respect for her grew. "I see you're looking for full-time or summer work."

"I need full-time work. But I know you hire extra people here for the summer, and that would suit me while I try to find a full-time job in the fall, or I might return to college and get my degree."

"What was your major in college?"

She hesitated. "My plans changed. I was studying communications. I thought about being a TV news reporter, but I doubt there are many openings for that. Now, I'm thinking in terms of teaching kindergarten or first grade."

He could visualize her as a news reporter. She had a good speaking voice. Very articulate. He liked her looks and her uncompromising stance concerning her commitment to the Lord.

She'd be a great addition to the organization. Just one problem. Two actually. One, he had hired all the workers he needed. The preschool and day-care workers had been there for years, and he didn't know of anyone planning to leave. The children's summer program workers had been hired months ago. Many returned from having worked the previous year.

They could always use extra help, but there was the matter of the budget.

He'd wondered if she might consider housekeeping or dining-hall work. But after talking with her, he doubted she'd be interested. Although those positions didn't require skilled training, other than what the organization offered, she definitely was over-qualified.

"I'm sorry." He spread his hands. "We don't have any openings in day care or the summer children's program. Or in any department for which you're qualified."

He really was sorry. She'd been fired because of her faith. Now she turned to a Christian organization for acceptance. He regretted seeing the hope in her hazel eyes turn to disappointment. "Thank you anyway." She rose from the chair and turned away.

Maybe. . .he shouldn't have made the decision about what kind of job she would accept. "Miss Jonsen."

She stopped but didn't turn toward him when he called her name. "We do have other departments and the possibility of a different kind of position opening up in a few weeks. If you'd be interested—"

She turned, and he saw the light of hope spark her eyes. Her dimple returned. Yes, he believed she was. . .interested.

૨ઢ

Ellen knew her delight was showing. She couldn't stop smiling.

Richard Williams said, "I'll be out showing Miss Jonsen some of the buildings, MaryJo," and walked ahead to open the door leading into the hallway.

Ellen said, "Bye," to MaryJo, who lifted her eyebrows and made a sign with her thumb and index finger indicating to Ellen that MaryJo knew something she didn't. Likely, the boss didn't usually walk out with a prospective employee.

When Mr. Williams opened the door, then looked around at them, MaryJo took on an innocent look and waved.

Ellen tried to look serious as she passed in front of Mr. Williams. He closed the door behind them and led the way down the hallway. While he pointed out various offices, Ellen glanced at the corresponding names and titles on the closed doors.

In the back of her mind, however, she thought about this man wanting to be a lion.

What characteristics did a lion have? King of the jungle. Well, in reality a lion might be called king of the jungle, but the animal and the jungle belonged to God. The lion just watched over his own territory in a masterful way. Yes, that might fit Mr.

Williams. He had the aura of a man in charge, one who knew his territory. But what did being "protective" of his territory mean? Don't invade it?

Somewhere she'd read that people saying they were a certain animal revealed something about their basic character— what they were, or sometimes what they were not but would like to be.

She had the impression Mr. Williams had lion characteristics. She could almost picture him like Mufasa in *The Lion King,* standing on a high rock overlooking his domain. Mr. Williams' position wasn't that high; however, he did have the aura of one who would elicit a second look.

Although he wasn't the most handsome man in the world—but then neither were most men on TV and in the movies who held such a distinction—she liked his looks. Nothing detracted, and she supposed her first impression was of a man in control, with dark hair, dark eyes, a conservative haircut, and wearing a conservative suit and tie. His shirt wasn't white though, but light blue.

She had the notion that the saying the eyes are the mirror of the soul held a lot of truth. She liked to watch a person's eyes as they talked. But during the interview, she got the distinct impression that Mr. William's dark eyes sought the same thing from her. His gaze seemed to penetrate her mind, as if he could read it.

That thought would have brought a blush if she were the blushing kind. She wouldn't want him to know she sat there analyzing him and considering him an attractive man. Not that it was wrong if the thoughts stopped there. Likely, a man who appeared to be in his mid-thirties was married or had someone special.

And she shouldn't be thinking that either. She was not looking for a man. She was looking for a job.

Almost before she realized it, they'd turned a corner, stepped into an elevator, and descended to the lobby where she'd come in.

Last week, she'd felt like the heavens were crying over her predicament. Today she felt as if a whole new world was opening up to her.

Mr. Williams paused for a moment in the spacious lobby, bright with sunlight from the tall windows. "We can sometimes use extra help with registration if there's a sudden increase in conferees," he was saying, as her glance swept up the staircase she had ascended earlier. Her gaze lifted higher to the top of the wooden-beamed cathedral ceiling with recessed lighting and great fans suspended from long golden chains.

"Miss Jonsen."

She returned her attention to him immediately.

"Shall we?" He moved to one of the glass doors with long panes separated by golden bars.

She stepped lively past the tall man. "Sorry. I was admiring the architecture. This building is beautiful. So are the others." She walked past him and onto the concrete porch. "The views are fantastic too."

He motioned down the long porch to his left, and she fell in step beside him as he asked, "Have you lived here long?"

"All my life," she admitted. "And I guess I take the mountains for granted to a certain extent. But never fully. It's always different. Each spring is like a new world." She liked the way he looked at her and smiled as if he knew what she meant. "And fall."

He nodded. "And summer. And winter."

"Exactly. And my being here is just another reminder of God's magnificent creation." She remembered the previous week's storm and how dismal everything had looked. One's outlook depended a lot on one's situation. But God's creation remained the same, even if one didn't appreciate it.

Mr. Williams must have sensed how she felt. He spoke of sitting in his office with his back to the view and how he could stare at it as it seemed to change daily. He laughed lightly. "I understand why I must sit facing a wall instead of the windows."

She laughed with him.

They walked down steps, up others, down a walkway, up steps again, onto another concrete porch, and into another building. "Rooms are in this building," he explained. "And also the cafeteria."

After walking down another long hallway, they entered the cafeteria, where he spoke to a couple of workers making coffee in huge urns. Then he led Ellen into a spacious dining room, filled with round tables that would seat six or eight. Only half the tables were spread with white tablecloths.

"We have a small conference in right now," Richard said. "Soon we'll be overflowing."

Ellen knew what he meant. The area was inundated with tens of thousands of people during tourist season. Would he offer her a job in the cafeteria?

As if she'd asked the question, he answered. "Right now we don't have any openings. But when the new hotel opens, and if we book additional conferences, we might need more help."

He led her out a back door, up more steps, past the bookstore, offices, gift shop, and up toward other buildings. "We use housekeepers in all the buildings, of course." He pointed out the various buildings that housed conferees.

"Up there is the new hotel," he said. "Do you think you'd be interested in a temporary, maybe even part-time job in the cafeteria or in housekeeping? Hey, we'd better move out of the middle of the street."

Ellen realized they'd come out the back way and were standing opposite the area where she drove to the preschool in the mornings. Parents were driving up. Others were already coming out with their children. She needed to answer his question. She couldn't honestly say she would like housekeeping or cafeteria work. But she could certainly accept that if nothing else were available. "That may be right for me at this time, since I'm thinking of returning to college in the fall."

"Would you like to see the hotel?" He laughed and added quickly, "When the traffic clears a little. It's not finished, but—"

She interrupted him with a shake of her head. "I would, but it's after four." She had picked up Missy at two all week, but today she'd received permission from Carol to leave Missy for day care. She saw a worker standing with Missy in the doorway. "I have to pick up Missy."

Before Ellen had time to explain, Missy saw her, broke away from the worker, and ran toward Ellen in spite of the worker calling her back. Ellen hurried across the street and toward the bridge to meet the little girl, afraid she might run out into the street.

"Mommy, Mommy!" Missy called.

Ellen laughed as Missy ran up, waving a bright yellow paper plate the size of a saucer while making a buzzing sound.

Bzzzzz. She turned the plate so a black triangle touched Ellen's arm. "You got stung."

Ellen pretended. "Ouch! Let me see that."

Missy held up the plate so she could see. "It has wings."

"I see." Ellen touched the translucent wings, made of waxed paper and taped onto the saucer. "That's a beautiful bee."

Suddenly, she realized that Richard Williams stood nearby, leaning back against the railing, watching them. Instinctively, she said what she'd normally say. "Now say hello to Mr. Williams." She glanced at Richard. "This is Missy. She's my—"

Being obedient, Missy said "Hello" before Ellen could complete her sentence, and Richard's action took Ellen by surprise. He knelt in front of Missy, balanced without his knees touching the floor of the bridge. How thoughtful that he'd stoop down to Missy's level.

"You wanna get stung by my bee?"

Richard laughed. "It would be an honor to be stung by such a fantastic bee."

"Bzzzz." She turned the bee so it stung his hand.

"Hey, he has eyes."

Missy's blond curls bounced with the nodding of her head.

Little flecks of sunlight danced in her blue eyes. "I colored them."

"Very nice. And it's very nice to meet such a pretty little girl, Missy. You have dimples, like your mom."

Missy corrected him. "She just has one. I have two."

"So I see," he said. His fingers touched the bridge to help with balance, then he stood.

Ellen realized how at ease he was with Missy. Did he have children? Not wearing a wedding ring didn't always mean a man wasn't married.

Missy tugged on Ellen's skirt. "Can we get some honey? Bees make honey."

"We'll talk later, Missy." She turned to Richard. "I can take Missy home and come back if you want me to see the hotel, or—"

He was shaking his head before she got halfway through the sentence. He looked around, acknowledging a couple of workers and a parent. His glance fell upon Missy, now exchanging bee stings with a little boy. He lifted his arm and looked at his watch, then back at her. "Well, I need to get back. My administrative assistant will be in touch. Thanks for your interest."

She nodded. "Thank you."

She wanted to tell him this could be an answer to prayer. She wanted to hug him right then and there for making it probable for her to have a job and for Missy to be in such a wonderful preschool that she loved already. She extended her hand.

He took her hand and released it almost as soon as he touched it. Nope, a hug wouldn't have done.

Heather had said, "He's a neat guy." Ellen agreed. She did get the feeling that he had a territory she mustn't invade. He was friendly, nice, but had an air of being in his own realm. She was very much aware that he was in charge, that he would make the decision of whether to hire her.

"It's been nice meeting you, Miss Jonsen."

She detected a slight pause before he hastily added, "You have a beautiful little girl there."

Suddenly, it dawned on her how this looked. She was a "Miss." But a child called her "Mommy."

seven

Ellen gazed after Richard Williams as he hastened down the road and strode across the concrete walk.

She loved Missy calling her "Mommy" instead of Ellen. She would not try to explain that away. It would be like a mother denying her own child. She couldn't call out to Richard Williams that she was not Missy's mommy, and she definitely could not say such a thing in front of Missy. She'd rather lose out on the job than hurt that child in any way.

"Come on, Missy. We need to go."

On the way home, Missy chattered away about what she'd done that day. Ellen listened, but at the same time, her thoughts drifted elsewhere.

She'd never forget when Missy had first called her "Mommy." It all began when Missy was three. The little girl had always called Ellen "Eh-wen," but then their mother died. Dad hadn't felt comfortable taking complete responsibility for a three year old. After seeking advice from her dad, friends, acquaintances, and the pastor, Ellen had finished the semester at the university, then hadn't registered for additional classes.

Her dad had encouraged to continue her education. "I'm grieving too, Dad," she'd said. "I'm sure it's in a different way than you. But I don't want to study. I just lost my mother. So has Missy. My school work doesn't hold the importance it held before Mom died."

He'd said they'd talk about it later. He hadn't protested during the next months, as Ellen took over the household chores and the primary care of Missy. "I love doing this, Dad," she'd said many times. He'd nodded and turned away. But not before she saw the moisture in his eyes. Almost daily he told her that he appreciated all she did.

Most days at some point, Missy would go from room to room, calling for and trying to find her mommy. When she cried for Mommy, Ellen was there. When she awoke from a dream or nightmare and called for Mommy, Ellen hurried to her. When she fell and wailed, "I want my mommy," Ellen consoled her. At times, Ellen let Missy sleep with her. Ellen understood. She had her own dreams about her mom, and a hollow spot was in her heart that nothing could fill. Mom had been a vital part of her life. Ellen felt Missy was handling the loss better than she and Dad.

They'd told the little girl often that Mom was in heaven with Jesus. They'd painted a beautiful word picture of heaven. "Can I go?" Missy had asked, her eyes wide with excitement.

"No, Darling. God wants us here until He's ready for us to die. God decides when He wants us to be in heaven."

Her little lips pouted. "I want to see Mommy."

"I know, Honey. Tell you what. Let's look at the scrapbooks and pictures. We will remember the good times we had with Mommy."

Ellen had hugged Missy. "I'll be your mommy."

She hadn't meant that Missy should call her that, but from that point on, Missy had started calling Ellen "Mommy." A few times, Ellen had explained, "I'm Ellen. Your mommy is in heaven."

Missy had looked at her with big blue eyes. She accepted whatever Ellen told her. But the next day at school, Missy had said, "Mommy, look what I did." And Ellen had stopped trying to convince Missy to call her "Ellen."

And now nothing would make Ellen call Richard Williams and explain the situation.

❧

Richard marched across campus, feeling the heat, not only of the bright afternoon sun, but from his quick stride and his frustration. He removed his suit coat and tossed it onto his shoulder.

Miss Jonsen had a child. One she hadn't bothered to mention.

Closer to the buildings, he strode along the concrete passage in the shade of the overhanging branches of oaks and maples. He wondered if he had overlooked something on her application.

He returned to the office. MaryJo had already gone. He went to his desk and looked at the application form. There were squares into which one could mark married, single, divorced, widowed. Under marital status, Miss Jonsen had checked "Single."

Had she been in such a rush on the day she filled out the application that she'd neglected to respond to all the questions? He saw the note from Carol. It seemed likely that Carol would have written the note after talking with Miss Jonsen about enrolling Missy in day care, rather than only talking with her about a possible job.

Why hadn't she mentioned her child? Having seen Miss Jonsen with the little girl, he had no doubt of the love between them.

If she'd never married, she possibly wouldn't feel comfortable talking about that.

He could understand that. Some things were best buried in the past. And he wasn't thinking only of Miss Jonsen. Things in his past were better left behind him.

However, those thoughts served no productive purpose, so he busied himself with jotting down some ideas he had about the new hotel dedication to be discussed at the next meeting of department heads.

Glancing at Miss Jonsen's folder that he'd laid aside, he told himself once again that while he could wonder, his place was not to judge.

eight

On Saturday morning, Ellen awoke at her usual early morning hour. Her dad almost always made whatever she and Missy wanted for breakfast. He'd done that when she was growing up, but he'd steered clear of household chores. Now, Daisy did most of those.

Saturdays were Ellen's time to catch up on all the things she couldn't get to during the week. Having a little girl around meant there was always laundry to do. Also, that was her only day for getting a haircut, buying personal items, and doing something fun with Missy.

Normally, she slept in for about thirty minutes or just lay in bed enjoying a short period of time before starting her hectic day of taking care of necessities and spending quality time with Missy. Often on Saturday, Missy came in to Ellen's bedroom, and they'd read books together in bed or watch a cartoon.

Ellen had too much on her mind to just lie there this morning. Besides, the smell of bacon frying in the pan and the voices of her Dad and Missy beckoned her into the kitchen.

Yawning, she walked into the kitchen and pushed her hair away from her face. "Mornin', Sugar Foot," she said to Missy. "Hi, Dad. Smells great."

Her dad returned the greeting. "The water's boiling for eggs. You want two?"

"That's great."

Missy looked up from the Barbie doll she was dressing. "Why you call me Sugar Foot?"

"Because you're so sweet."

"My foot is sweet?"

Ellen and her dad laughed.

"Sure."

"Just one of them?"

"No. I guess I could call you Sugar Feet."

Missy giggled. "You can call me Barbie."

Her dad brought the bacon to the table. Both Ellen and Missy reached for a piece.

He stood for a moment, and Ellen looked up, chomping on the bacon.

He said, "I'm taking Miss Sugar Feet Barbie here to that new Disney movie this afternoon."

Missy cried, "Ohhh," and rushed over and hugged him around the waist. "You're the bestest Pa-Pa in the world."

He patted the top of head. "You'd better tend to your Barbie and let me get back to the stove, or I'll be the worst cook in the world." The affection in his eyes, looking at Missy, touched Ellen's heart. They both needed that little girl so much.

Ellen swallowed the bite of bacon. "A movie sounds great. What time, so I can be ready?"

Her dad took an incredible length of time before answering. "Um, Miss Daisy's going with us."

"Oh." Ellen started to say, "The more the merrier," but something about the way he looked at her before turning away and walking to the stove gave her the impression she wasn't invited.

She talked to his back. "If you'd like, I can have supper ready when you get home."

He stirred the boiling eggs that didn't need to be stirred. "We'll just go to the cafeteria. Missy would like that."

Several questions popped into Ellen's head. Was she losing her mind, or was everybody turning against her? Was she doing nothing right anymore? Had she begun to take everything too personally?

"Well." She tried to sound cheerful. "Don't let her eat too much popcorn and candy."

He looked over his shoulder and peered above his eyeglasses. "I think I can handle this. I raised you, didn't I?"

Was this one of those kidding times. . .or was he repri-
manding her? *Don't be paranoid, Ellen,* she cautioned herself.
Take it as playful bantering. "Yeah. Mom always said that." She
laughed lightly. "But I loved that candy and popcorn. I'm glad
you didn't listen." She tried to mean that, although there was
more information around nowadays about too many sweets
than when she was growing up. And moms seemed more
cautious than dads about such things anyway.

But I'm not a mom. . .so everyone tells me.

When Dad left with Missy to pick up Miss Daisy, the last thing
he said to Ellen was, "Go out tonight. Have a good time."

Ellen stared after him. Go out? Where? With whom? The
idea of "going out" hadn't crossed her mind since her mother
had died. Her college-girl persona had died with her mother,
and a mature outlook on life had been born.

Although she missed her mom, she had dwelt more on
what Missy had lost. Ellen had years and memories. Missy
had just begun to know the mom who adopted her. Ellen had
tried to take her mom's place. Had wanted to.

And now, she was being constantly harangued by implica-
tions that she hadn't. . .or shouldn't.

Ellen went into the bathroom to straighten up. She
smiled and shook her head to see the wreck one little girl
could make of a room just by taking a bath. She dried off a
couple of toys and put them on the corner shelf, returned
the soap to its dish, and wrung out the washcloth and hung
it over a towel rack. She rinsed the tub with the shower-
head, put the bath mat on the side of the tub, then wiped up
splotches of water with the towel that had been tossed care-
lessly on the floor.

That done, she looked at the now-neat bathroom. A child
took a lot of time and effort. Sometimes it seemed there was
never enough time to keep up with the needs nor to give
Missy all the attention she deserved.

Ellen felt tears smart her eyes. The house was silent. No

TV. No little child. Just Ellen and her thoughts. She felt her mother's absence keenly.

No way would she trade that little girl of hers for something so meaningless as a clean bathroom, a silent house, a joyless life.

She needed to talk to someone.

After putting in a load of laundry, she called Heather, then made dinner reservations at the Chinese restaurant.

❧

"I know I've been a hard pill to swallow this past week, Heather." Ellen sat across from her friend at the restaurant. "You should be home studying."

Heather objected. "I need a diversion from all that required reading and studying. And you know, as much as I wanted the two of us to be roommates, I don't know if I would get through this master's deal if we were together all the time."

"Well, now, that's a fine howdy-do."

Heather laughed. "It's a compliment. We'd be out doing the town or yak-yakking all the time. The way it is, I'm either in class or holed up in my room at home, frying my brain. Oops! With required reading, I'm talking about."

They both leaned back as the waitress brought their menus and put glasses of water on the table.

"Oh, by the way," Ellen said after they had ordered. "Richard Williams is still the director of human resources at Ridgeway. He remembered you."

Heather grinned. "Well, haven't you realized I'm unforgettable?"

Ellen laughed lightly. "Actually, he implied that. He started to say something about you and got a weird look on his face like he was trying not to laugh. He definitely remembered something about you."

Heather cried out. "Oh, no!" She placed her hand over her mouth and looked around. A couple at a nearby table looked back curiously. She leaned toward Ellen and spoke in a lower tone. "I'm so sorry, Ellen. Maybe I shouldn't have been your reference after all. I didn't think he'd remember *that!*"

Ellen was puzzled. "What?"

"I told you about it. Jeff and I went for a hike and got lost."

"Oh yeah." Ellen cast her a teasing look. "You two were lost overnight, as I remember."

"Well, believe me, we held hands during that all-night trek. Good thing it was a clear night, although the forest was pretty dark at times. Anyway, Jeff called and had somebody from Ridgeway come and pick us up. Mr. Williams wanted to see us right away. After all, Jeff was a wilderness guide. He's not supposed to get lost. I think Mr. Williams was trying to find out if we were really lost or just took a hike for indiscreet reasons."

"Well, which was it?"

"Really, Ellen. What a question. Don't you know the answer?"

"Sure. Indiscreet reasons. You were crazy about Jeff."

Heather scoffed. "Now those dark patches of forest were interesting. But neither of us were crazy enough to deliberately spend the night in a snake- and bear-infested forest."

Ellen laughed. "You've lived an exciting life at times, that's for sure."

"Wait 'til you hear what I did to Patsy." Heather's gaze lifted to the ceiling and back again to Ellen. "I can't believe I did it."

"Oh, Heather. You didn't talk about me, did you?"

"Not directly. I didn't even go back for a week. I knew I had to have a cooling off period or I'd give her a piece of my mind. The worst piece, I might add."

Ellen smiled at her friend. She appreciated her loyalty. "It's not worth fighting over."

"She defended firing you, although I didn't attack her. I didn't accuse her of a thing. But the last thing I said to her was that Jesus loves her."

Ellen's mouth dropped open. She didn't know whether to commend or reprimand Heather. "That's the last thing she'd want to hear."

"I know. At first, I wanted to say something to get back at her. But I refrained. Since you and I were both open about being Christians, I knew I mustn't do or say anything to make Patsy have more to hold against Christianity. I didn't plan to say that, but when I did, the strangest thing happened. She became quite serious. I mean it. I really like Patsy. She's a good person and to be admired. She runs a great school."

Ellen agreed with that. "You think she thought you meant it?"

Heather shook her head. "Probably not. She fired you for singing 'Jesus Loves Me.' She could have thought I was being disrespectful."

The waitress set their food before them. They bowed their heads, and Ellen said grace. As soon as she finished and they'd both taste-tested and approved their food, Heather insisted Ellen tell all about the interview.

Between bites, Ellen told Heather how well things went until Mr. Williams met Missy. "I didn't even mention Missy during the interview. I didn't want him to think I was trying to push my way into a job by enrolling Missy in the preschool."

"Didn't you do that at Little Tykes?"

"Not really. Patsy was sympathetic about our situation with Mom dying and my needing to find a place for Missy, and I mentioned I'd be looking for a job. She initiated the conversation from there. She asked me to tell the story that first day, then I was a volunteer for quite awhile before she hired me. I didn't expect that. I don't want someone to give me a job out of sympathy, and I don't want it to look like I'm trying to manipulate my way into a job."

"But what's it going to look like if you don't explain about Missy? I mean, you said she called you Mommy."

Ellen took a deep breath and let it out. "It's going to look like I have a child who I didn't mention."

Heather nodded in agreement.

"Heather, there was a place on the application where one could list the names of children and ages. I am at such a loss in what to do anymore. I didn't have to do that with Patsy.

She knew my situation and that I was Missy's sister. I didn't put it on the Ridgeway application because legally Missy isn't my daughter. To put her down would look like she's my dependant or that I have sole responsibility for her, which would affect my working hours. That's not how it is. Dad can drive Missy where she needs to go. Or even Daisy." She made a helpless gesture with her hands.

"Ellen, do you think you should clarify the situation with Mr. Williams? How will he look at this? You didn't mention that you had a child. But a child called you Mommy?"

"Heather, I wish you wouldn't ask questions—just tell me what to do."

"I don't know what to do anymore than you, Ellen. I just wonder how it might affect him. How would it affect you?"

Ellen could answer that with immediacy. "Adversely."

"Maybe you should clarify it with him."

Ellen sighed. "You know, it's just the title 'Mommy' that causes any problem. Patsy called me a liar. Dad reminded me I'm not Missy's mom. I wish Dad would let me adopt her."

"Have you asked him?"

"No. The time never seems right. I didn't know for awhile if I could or should try and be Missy's mom. But I do know now. I wanted to wait until Dad got over Mom's dying. But Heather, he seems to be getting deeper into some kind of depression. There's something wrong. It's like he resents my mothering Missy, when he had appreciated it until recently."

"Talk to him."

Ellen nodded. "I'll have to. Even though he's not very receptive to anything I do or say nowadays."

❧

Jon Jonsen had to drive by his house when taking Daisy home. He glanced at his carport and stated the obvious, "Ellen's car isn't there. I guess she took my advice and went out for the evening."

That's what he'd encouraged her to do, but it made him uneasy. He understood it all too well. He was uneasy when

Ellen took over the role of mother to Missy, and he was uneasy at the thought of his taking over full responsibility.

"She needs to get out once in awhile, Jon."

After driving a few blocks farther, he pulled into Daisy's driveway. "Missy still asleep?"

Daisy looked back. "Dead to the world."

Jon switched off the engine. He could talk to Daisy. She'd been through losing a husband and understood how devastating that could be. At the same time, he wondered if it was easier for a woman. They could do so many things. "I've put too much responsibility on Ellen. It was easy to do after Mary died. Ellen just picked up with Missy where Mary left off. I don't know how to do that, Daisy."

She patted his hand. "You do fine, Jon. You two love each other. That's the important thing."

There was no denying that. "But Daisy. I have this heart valve thing that slows me down. The docs say it won't kill me if I take it easy. I'm not up to running after a little girl. And what happens in her teen years? I'm afraid I'm not the best person for her."

"You're a great Pa-Pa."

He nodded. "Yes, but not the dad she needs."

"There's Ellen. And she'll marry someday."

Jon sighed. "That's what worries me, Daisy. She doesn't go anywhere to meet anybody. And the field is now limited since she's taken on the care of Missy. It's just not right to let her do it."

He wished Daisy would contradict him. Or that his own mind could contradict him. But Daisy just sat there, squeezed his hand, and looked out at the darkening sky.

That was something he didn't like and did like about Daisy. She didn't tell him what to do when he needed somebody to do that. But he did like the fact they could just sit in comfortable silence.

"You never can tell how life's going to turn out," he said after a long moment. "Mary and I looked forward to my retirement from the post office. She was going to quit work too. Of course, we couldn't foresee that accident."

He continued reminiscing. "We were going to buy a camper and make payments on that. Take Missy with us and travel. See America." He scoffed. "I don't have to worry about money now. Life insurance took care of that. The house is paid off. I have a savings account, and nothing to spend it on."

Oh, he knew a lot of good could be done with that money, but he just had no sense of motivation in particular. He needed his heart to be in anything he did, and he felt like his heart had lost its capacity to feel. He touched his chest with his left hand. "I have a big rock where my heart used to be. Maybe it was buried along with Mary."

"I know how you feel." Daisy moved her hand away from his and onto her lap. "But the heart is an amazing thing, Jon. It has all those arteries and veins. And just imagine when one's heart isn't working right, they can go in there and clean out those arteries that keep the blood from flowing right. And think of all those bypass surgeries they do. They don't take the heart out. They just clean up what's messy or make a new path. The heart can handle a lot of redoing and be about as good as new."

"I was talking about emotions, Daisy."

"Well, so was I, Jon."

She smiled sweetly, said "Bye," and got out of the car.

Jon stared after her until she disappeared into her house and shut the door. His fingers tapped on the steering wheel. Sometimes that woman said the strangest things.

nine

First thing Monday morning, Richard spied Ellen Jonsen's folder on his desk. Whatever her personal situation, the fact remained that she needed a job. More than that, her child needed her mother to have a job. Now he understood why she wanted a job immediately and was willing to take anything, full time, part-time, or temporary. How difficult it must be to say, "I have a child, but I've never been married." She might think he'd stand in judgment of her.

Did he?

Most definitely!

He had very strong opinions about such matters. He greatly admired any single woman trying to support her child.

"Where should I file this one?" MaryJo asked upon seeing the folder still lying on the corner of his desk.

"This is a tough one, MaryJo. Apparently, she really needs a job and quickly. I can't use her in the preschool or day care. The summer program is set unless someone cancels, but we can't count on that. I think she'd probably take a housekeeping or cafeteria job, but I doubt she'd stay any length of time. It's not a good practice to hire someone you believe won't stay. Anyway, I can't use her there for a few weeks yet."

MaryJo grimaced. "Yeah. Too bad. I really liked her. I mean, getting fired for talking about your faith. Now that's something."

He thought so too. It spoke well of her. And it was often the failures people have that turn them in the right direction. MaryJo took his silence as not being able to offer a job to Ellen Jonsen. She picked the file up and headed for her office.

Richard prayed about his job. He wanted everyone working at Ridgeway to be in the will of God. He wanted his own life and work to be in God's will. He needed God's wisdom to make decisions, and none were too trivial to pray about.

He hadn't felt a peace about Miss Jonsen. That hadn't happened since the situation with a dining-room worker who told him she had breast cancer and would be taking treatments but needed to work and wanted to work as long as she could. He'd struggled with that. He'd known too many people taking those treatments who grew tired and weak. Would he be helping or hindering her by allowing her to continue working? Finally, he'd told her she could work as long as she was able.

That had turned out to be a wonderful blessing to everyone around her. When she became weak, the cashier exchanged jobs with her. Everyone who knew her situation, admired and respected her. She was a prime example of a woman of faith, ready to leave this world if God so chose, but determined to face each day with faith and joy.

He'd detected some of that kind of strength in Ellen Jonsen.

He wished he could help in some way. If he hadn't seen her child, he likely wouldn't feel so strongly about this.

God, let her find the right job. One You have picked out for her.

Determined to let it go, he turned to the papers on his desk.

He looked up when MaryJo returned to his desk. "I had a thought," she said.

He grinned. "Commendable."

She gave him a mock-mean look. "Really. I'm going to be out of the office for only three weeks after the baby's born." She tapped the folder. "You suppose she could fill in for me?"

Richard hadn't considered that. "You know we talked about calling the temporary secretarial service when you're ready to leave."

She shrugged a shoulder. "We didn't tell them that."

For some strange reason, this began to feel right. Miss Jonsen had said if she got temporary work, she might return to college in the fall. He nodded. "That could work to her advantage—and ours."

MaryJo opened the folder and looked at the application. "She has more skills than I had when I started the job. And it's not likely that the temp service has someone experienced in conference work."

He felt good about this. "Okay, let's give her a try. I'm not trying to rush you, but do you have any idea when you'll be leaving?"

"Yeah." She laughed. "As soon as I can be replaced. It's getting harder and harder to roll myself out of the bed every morning and waddle around here."

"All right. Call Miss Jonsen and see when she can come in. We'll give her and us a week to see how things go."

Richard stared at the door, even after MaryJo had gone into her office and closed it behind her.

Workers at Ridgeway were involved in God's work daily. What better place could there be for a young single mom?

His answer came in the form of a sense of peace.

❧

Ellen didn't want to go to the unemployment office just yet. She hoped she would be hired at Ridgeway for housekeeping or dining room at least for the summer. It might be a couple of weeks yet, but that would give her time to take care of household chores, some deep spring cleaning, take quilts and comforters to the cleaners, do any mending on hers and Missy's clothes. Missy had been experiencing a growth spurt lately and could use some new clothes. She was constantly growing out of her shoes.

After returning from taking Missy to preschool, Ellen encountered Daisy in the kitchen, washing breakfast dishes. Ellen's dad sat on the back deck, reading the morning paper. She pulled out a wrought-iron chair and sat next to him. She spoke softly, so Daisy wouldn't hear. "Dad, Daisy doesn't need to come while I'm not working."

He did not keep his voice low. "Ellen, I can't do that to Daisy. She is my housekeeper and cook. This job helps me and her. Now, do you really think it's fair to put her out of a job just because you lost yours?"

"Well, no, Dad. Not when you put it that way. I just thought maybe she'd like a break. And I can take care of things here."

He sounded as distant as his gaze that swept beyond her to the distant mountains. "I have a better idea. Why don't you go on a vacation? Or even take some summer courses at the university, or something. Ellen, you can go anywhere. I'll foot the bill."

He doesn't want me around anymore. No, don't go there, Ellen. Look at the positive side of what he's saying.

She took a deep breath and spoke as calmly as her emotions would allow. "You know, Dad, that may be a good idea. Missy doesn't have to be in preschool all the time." Ellen didn't think it a good idea to take Missy out of preschool when she was just getting adjusted to the change from Little Tykes. And how could she take a job and say she had to go on vacation first? But she wanted a right relationship with her dad. "Where would you like to go, Dad?"

The way he stared at his paper that she knew he wasn't reading said more than she wanted to believe. Then he said it in words. "No, Ellen. That's not what I mean. Oh, we can all take a vacation before Missy starts kindergarten if we want to. But what I mean is, while you're out of a job, why don't you go somewhere and have fun? Take Heather. Like I said, I'll foot the bill."

He wants me out of here. Why?

She didn't trust her voice, so she simply stood and laid her hand on his shoulder. He still didn't look at her. She dared say only one word. "Thanks."

≥

The call couldn't have come at a better time. Ellen had just splashed cold water on her face after shedding hot tears. Her heart and mind had called out to her mom. Things would be so different had her mom not died. That had changed everything—and her dad most of all. While she longed for comfort and assurance in his arms, she received only condemnation and a feeling that he didn't love her anymore. Did he want her to move out?

Lord, where are You in this? Are You leading? I feel like a lost sheep in need of a Shepherd.

After a deep breath, she tried a cheerful, "Hello."

"Ellen? This is MaryJo at Ridgeway."

Ellen held her breath for a moment. Was this a yes or no or what?

She released a grateful breath when MaryJo asked if she'd like to come in the next morning, on a trial basis, with the possibility of replacing MaryJo while she was on maternity leave.

As MaryJo talked, Ellen's eyes clouded, this time with tears of gratitude. God heard her prayers after all. He was answering. And this was only Monday morning. She'd lost her job on Thursday. Missy had started to school on Friday, she'd been interviewed the following Thursday, and now she had the prospect of a job that excited her even more than working at a hotel or in a cafeteria. She'd be working right next to someone who seemed to be what Heather had described as a "neat" guy—Richard Williams.

❧

On Tuesday as Richard approached MaryJo's office at nine, he heard voices. When he got to the doorway, he saw MaryJo and Ellen. They stopped their conversation and looked at him as he walked into the office and said, "Good morning."

"Oh, good morning," Ellen Jonsen replied, her words accompanied by a spark in her golden brown eyes and a dimple in her cheek that indicated she was quite pleased. "Thank you so much for this opportunity, Mr. Williams."

"My pleasure," he said. "We'll see how it goes this week and take it from there."

"Yes, Sir."

"MaryJo can fill you in on the basic requirements of the job. If you feel this job suits you, then come into my office before lunchtime, we'll talk, and I'll have you fill out the official forms."

She nodded. As he headed for his office, Richard heard MaryJo begin her instructions. "Let me show you what we have to enter on the computer. That will take up most of your time and concentration."

Richard entered his office and closed the door to give them more privacy. He'd thought of answering the phone himself, then thought better of it. That's something Miss Jonsen needed to learn too, regardless of how busy she might get.

Close to noon, she tapped on his door and spoke softly. "Mr. Williams. Would you like me to come in now?"

"Yes, that would be fine."

Although he wasn't sure he would have thought of her for this job without MaryJo's prodding, he felt good about the decision. He needed to feel that his job was a mission, with purpose.

MaryJo stood back at her desk, holding up her hand, forming an A-OK sign. She was a good judge of character. He'd come to appreciate the insight of a good assistant.

He had no doubt that Ellen Jonsen would do her best.

How good that was would be determined by the end of the week.

"I really appreciate this," Ellen said, even before she sat in the chair across from him, toward which he gestured.

Her eyes held a softness and warmth, full of appreciation. He smiled. Anyone liked to be appreciated.

"How's the instruction going?" he asked. "Is this something you feel you can handle and would like?"

He wondered if her hesitation meant he had asked too many questions at one time or if she had reservations. "I know it would take time for me to catch on to everything. MaryJo's a whiz."

Richard nodded. "True, but she had to learn. She's been here five years."

Ellen's dimple appeared, despite the wariness in her eyes. "I think the job is fascinating. Right now I feel overwhelmed, just because I don't know the routine. But MaryJo has a calendar of events, times, and schedules."

"We all have such calendars," Richard said. "Certain conferences and programs are basically the same during the summer, our prime season. Then, of course, we book new conferences, plan programs, and have to work closely with conference leaders and Ridgeway staff. Our summer youth staff is constantly changing since we employ a lot of college students. They graduate and go on to their careers. We plan some conferences. We assist organizations who plan their own."

Ellen was nodding. "MaryJo has written out so much for me. She's going to write more. I have a feeling much of my time will be taken up reading her notes."

"No one expects you to know everything right away. If you did, my job would be in danger." He hoped his words would dispel any concerns she had. "We all had to learn. And we're still learning. This is a place of both constants and change."

He heard her shaky intake of breath before she spoke. "Mr. Williams, if you think I can fill in for MaryJo, I'll do my best. I'll be honest; it is overwhelming. But I really want to try."

"Part of my job is to guide my assistant," he said. "If you can follow instructions, we should be fine. Of course, you can ask about what you don't know. And too, our volunteers will be trickling in soon. They're invaluable."

He talked to her about the business side of things, such as salary. She would not be entitled to benefits because of her temporary status. He wondered if she had any kind of insurance. He knew that children had periodic and unexpected visits to doctors.

She filled out the necessary forms for withholding taxes and signed the temporary job form that included the rest-of-the-week trial-basis clause.

She handed it to him. "Is that all?"

"Yes, thank you."

She stood. "MaryJo said to tell you we're going to lunch, if that's all right. She wants to start introducing me to the buildings and staff."

He nodded. "That's perfectly all right."

She returned his smile, then left the office.

Richard felt good about this situation. He swivelled around and stared at the old faithful mountainsides, now lushly green. Yes, God had a will for those who believed in Him. And it could be interesting sometimes, watching God work in His mysterious ways.

ten

Ellen squealed to Heather over the phone. "I got the job! I mean, at least I signed the contract that says I will be temporarily employed if I do okay during this week's trial basis. There's so much to learn, but I really want this job."

By the time she told her dad, she'd calmed down, cautious of his reaction.

Daisy had stayed for supper, during which Missy filled them in about the frog she'd made at preschool, complete with the ribbit-ribbits. Then Ellen told them all about the job.

"Goody, goody," Missy said. "You'll be working close to my school."

"That's right. I could pop in there anytime."

Everyone seemed excited for her. That is, until after Missy left the table to play with her frog. Daisy poured coffee.

The inquisition from her dad began almost immediately. "So, you have to prove yourself before the job is really yours?" he asked.

"Yes, Dad, but I know I can learn how to do the job."

"I have no doubt of that, Ellen. How long does this job last?

"For three weeks after MaryJo has her baby."

He sighed like she was a tremendous disappointment. "Then you'll go into housekeeping or cafeteria work, huh?"

On the defensive, Ellen shot back. "Dad, do you have something against housekeepers?"

He paused, glanced quickly at Daisy, and said, "Not if they're middle-aged women."

Daisy laughed. "He's lucky he didn't say 'old.' "

Ellen and Daisy laughed. Ellen's dad grinned, but he wasn't about to let this go. "I do have something against my college-aged daughter being a housekeeper instead of going to school."

Oh, not again! "Dad, I will register for the fall."

He blew on his coffee, then took a sip, peering over his eyeglasses. "And your boss? You like him?"

Ellen couldn't help but smile. "Very much. He's so nice."

"Is he single?"

Ellen glanced at Daisy, who grinned. They both knew what he was getting at. "Dad, MaryJo said he's never been married."

"How old is he?"

"I'd say mid-thirties."

"Something wrong with him?"

She really couldn't think of a thing wrong with him. "I don't think so, Dad. Just a confirmed bachelor."

Her dad nodded. "I was one of those until I was in my thirties. Then along came your mom. That 'confirmed' changed to 'eligible' right quick."

Ellen saw the shadow cross his face as he whispered, "We had a good life. I miss that." He looked down at his food and moved it around on his plate with his fork.

Daisy broke the silence. "Jon, I'm ready for you to plow my garden if you still want to. Won't be long 'til planting time."

The food suddenly seemed tasteless to Ellen as she watched her dad seem to drift off into another world. Daisy kept talking about planting cool-weather crops first, like spinach. Her dad's moodiness wasn't good for her, and it certainly wasn't good for Missy.

After supper, while her dad watched the news on TV in the living room and Missy played on the swing set in the fenced-in backyard, Ellen helped Daisy with supper dishes. Maybe she could offer some advice.

"Daisy, do you think Dad is regressing?"

"Re—?" She looked at Ellen as if she were the one who had lost her mind. "What do you mean, Honey?"

"I don't know if he just can't get over Mom's dying or what. But he seems so different lately. And he's always at me to enroll in college."

Daisy talked as she scrubbed at spots on the table, invisible to Ellen. "You're under his roof, Ellen. My advice is do as he asks."

That wasn't what Ellen expected. *Under his roof?*

The implication made Ellen feel the same as she had so often lately when talking to her dad. Maybe he wanted her to move out.

Daisy walked closer to Ellen, glanced at the living-room doorway, then spoke in a low tone. "Now I'm not saying he would make you move out, but you need to consider the possibility." She lifted her hands in a surrender gesture. "Now I'm not saying he would. But he is your dad."

That left no doubt in Ellen's mind about whose side Daisy was on, if one were taking sides.

Maybe Daisy could offer some advice in another area.

"Sometimes I feel he doesn't. . ." Ellen's voice broke as she tried to say it. "Doesn't love me anymore."

"Oh, now, Honey, don't ever think that. Sometimes children don't understand when parents are using tough love."

Ellen wanted to scream that she wasn't a child. She was a twenty-four-year old adult taking on the responsibility of a mom. But it wouldn't do any good to say that to Daisy. Nor to her dad, who would simply say, "You're not Missy's mom."

Daisy touched Ellen's arm. "Your dad has loved you for twenty-four years. That hasn't changed, except to grow deeper and stronger."

Ellen attempted a smile. But if her dad still loved her, tough or otherwise, then why didn't she feel it?

ೊ

Ellen felt great on the job from the time she stepped into MaryJo's office each morning for the rest of the week. In addition to MaryJo's notes, Ellen took some of her own. She realized that a lot of the job did not require initiative on her part but rather responses to upcoming events. She attended a staff meeting and took notes on an event being planned. She answered the phone and learned to check the calendar and the computer for pertinent information.

MaryJo often asked Richard questions about events. He, in turn, informed her of things that needed attention. On Thursday afternoon, MaryJo helped at the registration desk for a conference. After watching for awhile, Ellen registered conferees while MaryJo looked on.

"You don't have to do this often," MaryJo said, "but sometimes an emergency occurs and a worker can't be here. We pitch in wherever needed, whenever possible."

Ellen liked that spirit of cooperation.

And as much as she loved children, she discovered she also loved relating to adults for a change. She realized she'd never related in exactly this way before. She'd been a college student with studies primarily on her mind, then had the responsibilities of caring for a little girl. She believed Missy's welfare must come first and that meant more to her than any job. But she did enjoy being a part of the workplace and feeling that she was making a contribution to a worthwhile organization.

On Friday, Richard asked MaryJo to have lunch with him. Ellen had a strong feeling he wanted to ask MaryJo's opinion of her ability to handle the job for a few weeks. Ellen stayed in the office.

For an hour, Ellen told herself not to be nervous. She'd made no terrible boo-boos during the week that she knew of. MaryJo had been a good teacher. She had a lot to learn, but she'd proved herself capable of learning.

MaryJo returned alone.

Ellen whispered. "Is he coming in?"

"He who?"

"MaryJo, don't tease me. I know you guys had to be discussing me."

"Right. But he likes to be the one to break the news—good or bad."

"And you can't tell me if it's good or bad."

If anyone ever had a "happy face," it was MaryJo. Ellen thought if the news were bad, she'd see sympathy or regret in MaryJo's expression. Now MaryJo turned away.

Ellen decided she would not look at Mr. Williams when he came back into the office. If he called her in and said he didn't think she was right for the job, she wouldn't ask "Why not?" She wouldn't cry. She wouldn't beg. She wouldn't run out the door—or the window!

Or would she?

She felt like a downpour was about to happen just thinking about not fitting in here. She loved it. She liked relating to MaryJo each day on an adult level.

"I've gotta run down the hall a minute," Ellen said after another hour had passed. She grimaced. "Nerves."

MaryJo nodded.

Walking briskly toward the door, Ellen looked back over her shoulder at MaryJo. That was just long enough to hear a yelp of "Ho oh!" from the doorway. She turned to find herself eye-to-tie with Richard Williams. She looked up.

All she could think of in that moment of eternity, about two inches away from him and staring up into his face, was that his eyes held an expression of. . .was that mischief?

"Hey," he said, raising his arms in an "I surrender" position. He held a waxed-paper-wrapped bouquet of flowers in each hand. "I always bring flowers to my administrative assistants, temporary or not, but you don't have to fight me for them."

She heard MaryJo's burst of laughter, but her mind was registering his saying "my assistants," plural. Did that mean she was definitely hired?

Oh, she could hug him! She squelched the urge.

He handed a bouquet of red roses to Ellen. "Welcome aboard. That is, if you take the job."

She could cry. Instead, she said, "Yes," and thanked him. He handed the other bouquet to MaryJo.

"For me?" MaryJo smelled the roses. "Whatever did I do to deserve this, Richard?"

"Nothing at all," he said, as if he meant it. "I'm teaching that son of yours a lesson. If there are two women in an office, never dare to bring flowers to only one."

MaryJo nodded vigorously. "You're very smart, Richard."

He laughed. "I know. That's why I'm the boss."

MaryJo looked at Ellen and mouthed, "He thinks."

Ellen was surprised at his bringing flowers. All week, things had been business-like between them.

"Is there a vase?" she asked.

"Why don't we take them home, since it's the weekend." MaryJo looked at Ellen. "I think you can handle things without me, Ellen. The doctor said I need to stay off my feet. This close, I don't want anything to go wrong. Richard may not know the answers, but you can call me at home if you need me."

He picked up her bouquet. "I'll just take these back."

MaryJo grabbed for them. "Oh, no, you don't."

Laughing, he returned the bouquet to the desk. "By the way," he said, "to celebrate MaryJo's departure and your staying, Ellen, I'm throwing an impromptu cookout at my house tomorrow. Come around four or five. I have a pool. You might like to swim."

"Uh oh," MaryJo said. "That 'impromptu' means BYOF!" She looked askance at Ellen and mumbled, "Bring your own food."

"MaryJo, that's not true. I'm providing the meat—steaks, hamburgers, hot dogs."

"And we just bring the accessories."

"That's all."

Ellen liked the friendly bantering between the two. He glanced from MaryJo to Ellen, the light of humor still dancing in his dark eyes. "MaryJo can give you directions to my place."

"Thank you, Mr. Williams. For. . .everything."

He smiled, and she felt like he had truly given her everything.

"You're welcome," he said. "And feel free to bring a friend. There will be some couples and some singles. And if the word gets around, some party crashers."

She laughed with him. "Thank you."

"Bring Missy if you like. My friend Jerry will likely come and bring his son, Jacob. He and Missy look about the same age. He may even be in her class at preschool."

"I've heard the name," Ellen said. She didn't, however, know which child was Jacob.

After he went into his office and closed the door, Ellen laid her roses on MaryJo's desk. "I know you said he was generous and had a sense of humor, but that's the first I've seen of it."

"He's very serious-minded on the job. I've kind of caught on when he's in the joking mood. Ellen, he's really a great guy."

"I guess so, if he always gives his new employees roses."

"This is news to me." MaryJo's eyebrows moved upward. "I don't remember any flowers when I came to work here. I get a feeling he's not at all sad that I'm leaving." She grinned as if expecting a reply from Ellen.

Ellen headed for the door. "Gotta go. Nerves."

eleven

While she arranged the roses in a vase, Ellen told her dad about the cookout.

"That's nice," he said. "You can leave Missy with me."

"But Dad, other children will be there. She'd love it. Mr. Williams said I could bring a friend. It's fine if you want to go with me."

"Ellen, I'm Missy's dad. She calls you Mom. You're my daughter. How's that going to look? We have to go through all those explanations, if anybody dares ask."

Is that what had been bothering him? Ellen had never thought of it in that way. "Dad, I can easily say she's my sister. Missy knows she's adopted and that I'm her sister. She just wants to call me Mommy. Maybe I was wrong to let her do that. But when she lost Mom, she transferred that title to me. It just seemed right at the time."

"Yes," he agreed. "To me too. But now. . ." He shook his head. "I'm re-thinking the whole situation. I think some changes need to be made."

"So do I, Dad. I don't know if this is the time to say it, and. . . it's nothing against you. But would you consider letting me adopt Missy?"

He stared as if she'd struck him. Couldn't he just say no without looking as if she'd committed a crime?

Finally he spoke. "That's not at all what I have in mind, Ellen."

She hugged her arms to herself, feeling a chill.

Her dad turned and walked away.

What did he have in mind?

❧

Saturday morning, Jon went to Daisy's and began tilling her

garden spot. He paused and wiped sweat from his brow on his sleeve as she brought out two glasses of lemonade. They sat in wooden chairs on the back deck. He told her about the cookout.

"Now, Jon. It's a beautiful day. It's Saturday. How could you think Missy shouldn't go to that cookout?"

"I don't know what to do anymore. What's best. What's right. I pray. I try to listen, but. . .I don't know. That job has made a huge difference in Ellen. Kind of like a lightbulb was turned on inside her. She loves the job. She likes her boss. And that's good. Ellen should be thinking of herself. Her own future, instead of only Missy."

"She can't, Jon. She took Mary's place with that little girl."

"I know. But none of us could foresee how this would play out." He had already told Daisy much of the story. Mary's niece, Leanne, at age fourteen had become pregnant. Neither she nor her mom could care for the baby properly, and they had planned to put it up for adoption. Mary took Missy to keep her from being adopted by strangers. She thought Leanne might change her mind after she grew up a little.

"Mary and I fell in love with Missy but considered ourselves foster-grandparents. Then Leanne went back to school, got into activities, got the lead part in the school play. A year passed. Leanne's mom said Leanne was getting on with her life and something had do be done legally. Mary wanted to adopt her," Jon said. "She was part of our family. I went along with it. Our grandchildren called us Ma-Ma and Pa-Pa. Before we adopted Missy, that seemed the best title for us. After the adoption, I thought it best for her to continue calling me Pa-Pa. Mary began to call herself Mommy to Missy."

He sighed. "Is Ellen right and am I wrong? Oh, I know we're responsible for that little girl, and I love her with all my heart. But am I right for her?"

"Jon, that child loves you."

"I know. I'm her Pa-Pa. I'm even more of a Pa-Pa to her than to my grandchildren since we adopted her. But suppose

Ellen wasn't in the picture? What then? I mean, Mary took care of little girl things. I wouldn't know if Missy needs a haircut or how to make a ponytail or when she should or shouldn't get her ears pierced and things like that."

"But Ellen is here."

"Suppose she wasn't? Would you be willing to take on that kind of responsibility day-after-day, day-in and day-out?"

He thought she'd never answer. He didn't seem to be getting through to anybody nowadays. Finally, she looked him in the eye with that composed expression of hers.

"Jon, you have to find your own answers to how you will live your life. And about Missy."

He scoffed. "Daisy, God's supposed to speak through people. You're a big one on prayer. I thought He might've told you something."

She got that huffy look as she straightened her shoulders and scooted her chair back from the table. "Jon, God tells me my answers. Not yours."

She lifted her lemonade to her lips as he mumbled, "Thanks a lot!"

Well, that got him nowhere. He'd try again. "Ellen should be out finding herself a husband instead of being a mom."

Daisy answered quickly. "She loves that child as much as you, Jon."

"I know. But it's not fair to her. If Ellen wasn't around, what kind of dad would I be? Just me and Missy? Am I best for her? I'm not very exciting."

The next thing he knew, Daisy reached across the table and laid her hand on his. She spoke in that soft way of hers. "Now, Jon, don't put yourself down that way. 'Exciting' depends upon one's definition, I suppose."

Daisy got up and took their empty glasses into the house.

Jon went back to his plowing, trying to figure out Daisy's unexpected "exciting" response.

❧

Richard couldn't have ordered a better day for a cookout. Who could ask for more than a day in the mid-seventies, a cool breeze, and a clear sky, accompanied by his spectacular view?

Maybe one thing—it would be nice if Ellen showed up, since he'd planned this primarily for her and MaryJo.

Just as he was about to give up on Ellen's coming, he saw a little tow-headed girl in shorts and shirt, with a tote bag over her arm, run around the side of his chalet. She stopped, stood with her hands on her hips, apparently surveying her surroundings through her sunglasses that had some kind of female figure on the rims. Looked like one of those Barbie-type dolls. He smiled. She was a little beauty.

And her mom's nothing to sneeze at, he thought as Ellen came up behind Missy. He shook away that thought. Yes, she looked quite nice in denim jeans and a green T-shirt.

Then he realized someone was with her. Richard stepped away from the grill and walked toward them. "Welcome," he said. "Hello, Missy. You look like a swimmer to me."

She sighed heavily. "Yes." She looked toward the pool. "If it's not too deep."

"It's deep," he said. "But right over there are floats, life jackets, and boards you can hold onto."

She smiled. "Okay."

"Hold it!" Ellen's words stopped Missy as soon as she turned toward the equipment. "You wait for me. We've already talked about this."

Missy sighed again and turned toward the pool, watching the activity.

"Mr. Williams, this is my friend, Heather—"

Heather interrupted. "Oh, Richard and I have met before."

He laughed with her. "Yes, Miss Cannington. I believe we have." He really hadn't remembered what Heather had looked like, except he'd thought of her as a rather gangly teenager. She'd grown into a lovely young woman.

"Oh," she said. "I slaved over a hot stove all day cooking these potato chips."

He recognized the store-bought brand. "Thank you. Here,

put them on the table. I don't use bowls. Just open the bag."

Ellen set down her dish and lifted the edge of the foil. "I did cook these."

"Brownies?" They must still be warm. He could smell the chocolate.

"With walnuts," she said. She looked up at him. Her cheek dimpled. Her eyes looked green.

He reached over and pinched off a big chunk. "I have to test these. Make sure they're okay."

"Well?" she queried.

Well what? Oh, the test. For a minute there he forgot anything but realizing she stood there, gazing at him with brown eyes touched by the golden glow of a sunny summer day.

"Oh. Can't tell. I'll have to try again."

Her dimple appeared. "You're the boss."

He corrected her. "Only in the office."

"In that case. . ." She pushed the corner of the foil down just as his fingers reached for another bite. "Dessert later," she said playfully, as if she were speaking to Missy.

He liked this relaxed Ellen. In the office, she'd been reserved. But then, that's what cookouts were for—to make friends and influence people. "Here," he said, "I want you to meet Jerry."

She turned around to where he gestured.

Jerry, Ridgeway's graphic artist, had tied a short beach robe around his waist and had just walked up. He stood near Heather and Missy. His curly auburn hair looked like a rust-colored mop that hadn't been wrung out. Pool water dripped down his face. "I'm Jerry," he said in greeting, "and this is my son, Jacob."

Missy nodded. "He's in my school."

Jerry took over from there. "I'm the official lifeguard," he told them. "But first, let's go meet everybody."

Richard returned to the grill and lifted the huge lid. The hot dogs were ready. Hamburgers and steaks had a way to go yet. Placing the hot dogs in the warming bin, he smiled, observing his guests. MaryJo sat on the edge of the pool with her feet in the water, while Ben swam side-by-side with Ken, the youth pastor at the church Richard attended. Ken's girl-friend hadn't been able to come.

Leon and Sue, good friends who were a few years older than he and managed the bookstore, sat in lounge chairs. They had teenagers at home and said they just wanted to sit, observe, and relax. Near them lounged Jerry's administrative assistant and her husband. They'd recently welcomed their first grandchild into the world.

Jerry took Ellen, Heather, and Missy around and intro-duced them, then fitted Missy and Jacob with life jackets and got them into the pool. After speaking to everyone, Ellen pulled up a chair near MaryJo at the poolside, talked to her, and watched the children. Soon, Ken swam over and talked with her.

After they all sat down to eat, Richard observed Heather's outgoing personality, like Jerry's. Heather told about getting lost overnight with Jeff when she was a teenager, and they all laughed. She talked about her master's thesis that included research at Little Tykes and inclusion of the Ridgeway preschool.

Ellen had no problem relating to everyone, but she did have to divide her attention between them and her daughter. Missy and Jacob had chosen to sit at a picnic table apart from the others at the long table.

He could understand how Ellen and Heather would be friends. They said they'd known each other since grade school. Heather had been a cheerleader, outgoing. Ellen had been the president of the student body, more academic.

Heather's taking courses in child development in order to learn more about the children's books she wanted to write was impressive. She laughed and said, "I picked a thesis that Miss Academia could help me with. I'd never have gotten this far without Ellen. Never learned how to study. Tell them your formula, El."

"Six steps," Ellen said, counting them off on her fingers. "Sit down, shut up, read, take notes, reason them through, and apply them to memory."

Heather sighed. "She's a tough taskmaster."

They all laughed. Ellen shook her head. "Don't let her fool you. You have to have brains and apply them to get through college and into a master's program.

"Did you go to UNCA too, Ellen?" Ken asked.

"I did, but I dropped out in my senior year to take care of Missy."

"I'm sorry I didn't have a permanent position to offer." Richard tried to manipulate the conversation without prying. "I'm sure it's quite expensive raising a child."

Heather spoke up quickly. "Oh, Ellen's not the financial support for her sister."

Ken spoke up. "Missy's your sister?"

Richard noticed that Ellen didn't quite meet anyone's eyes. She looked very uncomfortable.

Heather answered for her. "Now there's something to be praised," she said. "After her mom died, Ellen has taken care of her little sister like she was her own child."

Little sister?

Richard stared at Ellen a moment longer. As if feeling his stare, her gaze locked with his. Then she looked toward Missy.

Missy had said, "Mommy."

Heather said, "Sister." And that she'd lost her mom. Did she still have her dad? Obviously, she'd put her own future on hold for her little sister.

The more he knew of Ellen Jonsen, the more Richard admired her.

And the more a nagging uneasiness began to grow deep within himself.

❧

Ellen hadn't had a crush on a guy since high school. She liked the academic type, like the gorgeous boy who'd edited the school paper and played a saxophone in the band. Not that she had a crush now, but that came to mind when Mr. Williams brought out his drums and Jerry his guitar.

She could almost forget thinking about Mr. Williams as her boss. She could easily see him just as a man she really liked. He and Jerry sang a silly song and taught it to them all. Heather suggested they sing a popular Christian song and pulled Ellen in on it.

Her alto and Heather's soprano blended well with Richard's and Jerry's voices, accompanied by the drums and guitar. Then Heather sang a song with a mock nasal country sound. Everyone loved it.

All had their turn at singing. Some attempts caused hands to be placed over ears. Missy and Jacob had joined in, complete with clapping.

"I can sing 'Froggie Went a Courtin','" Missy said. "Pa-Pa sings it to me a lot."

She sang the two verses that she knew, bobbing her head when she emphasized the "uh-huh, uh-huh" part.

"One more time!" Richard said. "And we'll all sing the 'uh-huh's. Lead us, Missy."

She shook her head, becoming suddenly shy.

"I'll sing it with you." He started, "Frrrrr. . .roggy. . . ," and looked at Missy who glanced away from him as if to say he'd ruin it. He continued, then she began to sing along with him.

Richard gestured with his hands, as if pulling them all toward him. They all joined in with the "uh-huh, uh-huh's" along with a few "ribbits."

At the end, while everyone followed with laughter and applause, Richard put his arm around Missy's shoulder and pulled her gently to his side. She looked up at him with her big blue eyes. Ellen thought the way they related indicated a mutual liking. How wonderful if Missy could have a dad like Richard.

Immediately, she felt she'd done a disservice to her own dad. But she hadn't meant to think of it that way. Her dad was the most wonderful man alive. She loved him more than any man in the world. And she'd always admired and respected him. He had no major flaws. He had his human imperfections, but who didn't?

Her dad didn't have the energy, or the inclination, to be the kind of active dad that he'd been to Ellen. And his desire to do so had waned in the past couple of years. That was understandable. Missy had been her mom's major responsibility before she died, not his.

Ellen observed that Missy left Richard's brief embrace and ran off with Jacob and Rachel, who hopped up and walked along the top of the rock wall several feet high that surrounded the patio. However, strangely, the world around her seemed to have faded into the background while she stared into Richard's eyes. How long had she stared before he turned to another guest?

Before long, some of the guests were leaving. Jerry was supervising Missy and Jacob throwing a rubber ball back and forth, near the pool.

Next thing Ellen knew, Heather brought her a cup of coffee and sat beside her.

"Imagine. You and I without a man and right here are three eligible bachelors."

Ellen remembered what her dad had said about eligible and confirmed. "Maybe they're confirmed."

Heather scoffed. "That means he's tenacious about remaining a bachelor. But you know another saying—he runs, until she catches him."

"Who's trying to catch anybody?"

Heather bumped her shoulder against Ellen, almost making her coffee spill. "Ellen, this is me. We're red-blooded American girls, and there's nothing we'd like better than to find Mr. Right."

Ellen sighed. "Does he exist?"

"Well, these ain't bad. But at the moment, I'm knee deep in a master's thesis. Can't handle a man."

"Well, I'm waist deep in a child. So I know what you mean."

Heather burst into laugher. "Yeah. Means we don't have anyone head over heels about us."

Ellen agreed. But she didn't want to spoil a good working relationship by letting her mind take off on some fantasy trip. Richard Williams was her boss, a confirmed bachelor who'd hired her to fill in for a few weeks. How eligible was anybody anyway? "I don't know Jerry's situation, and I heard Ken has a girlfriend. And Mr. Williams and I," she emphasized, "are not even on a first-name basis."

She looked around. "We'd better go. We're almost the last ones left."

Just then, she felt someone sit on the bench beside her.

The surprise of it made her heart beat faster.

Heather said, "I'll get Missy." She ran off.

Ellen glanced over at Richard. "Thank you so much, Mr. Williams, for inviting me. Missy had a great time." She laughed lightly. "So did I."

"I'm glad. But let's get one thing straight. Here, I'm just Richard. You may have noticed that when we're not conducting business, even in the office, MaryJo calls me Richard. May I call you Ellen?"

"Oh, please do," she said, feeling a rush of excitement like a high school girl when the saxophone player just says, "Hi." She really had been out of circulation for a long time.

She looked down from his smile and at her coffee cup. Heather's words—"Mr. Right"—rang in her ears, along with a delicious thought.

Richard and I are on a first-name basis.

twelve

When Richard arrived in Ellen's office at nine, she was talking on the telephone.

"Yes, I will give Mr. Williams the message. Good-bye." She hung up and sounded very professional as she looked at the note she'd taken and explained to him, "Daniel Smith's mother called. Due to circumstances beyond their control, Daniel will arrive here a day later than scheduled."

Richard nodded, watching the becoming color rise to her cheeks. "And what do you plan to do with that information?"

"I just told my boss," she said, then grimaced as if she might have said something wrong. To reassure her all was fine, he nodded and smiled.

"And too," she said, her dimple showing, "I will put a note in his file, and I will contact the summer staff director's office." She gazed at him with her eyes wide, waiting for approval.

"Very efficiently handled." He saw the disappointment in her face when he added, "You've done only one thing wrong this morning. We begin our day with a little informality. So let's start over. Good morning, Ellen."

"Good morning."

He cupped his ear with his hand, and she added, "Richard."

That's the first time he'd heard her say his first name. He'd only meant to be friendly and put her at ease. Instead, the tentative way she softly said his name, in almost a whisper, touched something deep inside him and elicited that uneasiness again.

But he had neither the time nor inclination to explore why he had reacted in that way. Work awaited. "First on the agenda," he said, "we should tour the new hotel. I'd like for you to be a tour guide at the dedication."

"Tour guide?" She looked doubtful. "I get lost going from the cafeteria to the bookstore."

"It's only a tour of the hotel. So if you'll put the phone on answering machine, we can go."

After they walked out a back door of the administration building and across the concrete pathways, he noticed her gaze moved to the day-care center, as if wanting to see Missy. "At the cookout, Heather mentioned your mom dying. I'm sorry."

"Thank you," she said softly.

"Do you have a dad?"

"Yes, Missy and I live with him." She briefly mentioned the accident that killed her mom. She talked of her parents' having adopted Missy at birth.

He already knew Ellen was special. But this was even more remarkable. She loved Missy like a daughter although they were not blood-related. With all the negativity in the world, how wonderful to be reminded of the goodness in some people.

She asked about his parents.

"They live in Raleigh," he said. "My dad has an accounting business. They both work there. They come here for conferences occasionally."

They reached the covered entry, bordered by newly planted blooming flowers, lush green plants, and bushes. The hotel rose four-stories high and was surrounded by exquisite mountain views.

"It smells so clean and new," Ellen said upon entering the hallway with offices on each side and a spacious area in the center where hallways were located to the left and right. Long windows formed the wall across from them, exposing the panoramic view of one mountainside after another.

More beautiful, however, was the young woman beside him, taking in the grandeur of a newly built structure. He led the way to the auditorium, where more than two hundred chairs, each with its own desk that could be raised or lowered to the side, faced the glass window that reached from the floor to the high-beamed ceiling.

"All the latest equipment," Richard pointed out as they went into classrooms and saw panels with switches, computerized buttons, and electrical sockets set flush with the wall. "State-of-the-art technology," he said.

He showed her the board room.

"Impressive," she said, touching the polished wooden table surrounded by twelve high-backed leather chairs. She drew in her breath and walked over to a painting. "He Lives," she said, reading the title of the painting of Peter and Andrew. "That's. . ." She paused as if searching for the right word and then said, "Awesome."

Richard agreed. The look on the disciples' faces as they gazed at something not shown in the painting, but likely the Christ Himself, held pure awe.

They rode the elevator to the upper floors, walked across the brown-and-beige carpet, bordered by a darker brown strip on each side, and explored VIP rooms, fellowship rooms, and banquet rooms.

When Richard finished the tour, he said, "Okay. Now it's your turn. Give me a tour."

As he followed her, he listened to her and watched her look at him with little golden flecks of mischief in her eyes as she performed her serious mission. He could see she liked a challenge. When she returned to the painting, her expression changed to reverent appreciation.

"Oh," she exclaimed when they returned to auditorium. "I remember there are two hundred chairs in here, but I forgot how many guest rooms there are."

"One hundred twenty," he said. "But all that will be written out on the programs given to everyone."

She gave him a now-you-tell-me look that made him laugh. Working around Ellen was going to be easy—and difficult.

❧

On Tuesday morning, MaryJo's husband burst into the office. "Guess what! Guess what!"

Richard almost ran into Ellen's office, then stopped and

laughed. "Ben, I can't imagine. As if that euphoric look on your face says nothing. Not to mention what you're waving around in your hand.

Ben laughed. "I think you guessed it. Tyler has arrived!" He pulled out two pieces of bubble gum wrapped in blue paper from the bag he held. He handed a piece to Ellen and one to Richard. "It was hard on me," he said, "but MaryJo's fine. Tyler weighs eight pounds, six ounces, is twenty-two and one-half inches long, and has terrific lungs."

After Ben left to deliver more bubble gum and spread the news to others, realization struck Ellen. This meant her job would end in three weeks. Her quick glance at Richard revealed he wasn't smiling either. Did he think the same thing? Did it matter? Was he looking forward to MaryJo's return? He looked down and fingered the bubble gum.

Three weeks.

The idea of working in housekeeping or the cafeteria had lost all appeal since she'd been working with Richard. She'd been totally happy with the job and felt she'd done well. Now a creepy, desolate feeling washed over her. She tried to shake it.

"Richard." She hesitated. Two weeks ago he was Mr. Williams. Now the name Richard rolled off her tongue without hesitation. And she liked the way he said her name. How could she ever like another job? But she mustn't think that. She hoped her voice didn't betray how her emotions were trembling. Uncanny how one's outer demeanor could reveal what lay beneath the surface. "I'll go see MaryJo after work. Want me to tell her hello for you or anything?"

Whatever emotion had caused his frown vanished. He chuckled, stuck his bubble gum into his pocket, walked over and balanced his hands against the edge of her desk, and leaned toward her. He made his face look grim, but his eyes were smiling. "Are you trying to tell me I should send flowers or something?"

MaryJo had told Ellen she would need to remind Richard about special events that weren't directly business related. He tended to forget some of those. This might be one of those times. She jested with him, as MaryJo had done. "That would be nice, Richard," she said playfully. "She is your administrative assistant."

After a moment's hesitation, he said, "She was. She will be. But for the present. . .you is."

She couldn't help but laugh. "I is?"

"That's what I said, and I'm the boss. I might add I'm very pleased with you. With your work," he said, with a look that warmed her heart.

She couldn't look away. "I like this job."

He nodded and looked as if he were about to say something more when the door opened and Jerry walked in, holding out a piece of gum in the palm of his hand.

Jerry must have wondered what Richard was doing, leaning over her desk. Ellen saw his quick glance from one to the other as Richard straightened. Jerry gestured toward Ellen's piece of gum. "I see the happy father has been here too."

"Right. How's it going, Jer?" Richard asked.

"Great. My boy's turning five this weekend." He pulled an envelope from his pocket and handed it to Ellen. "I told him he could invite a few friends and we'd go to putt-putt. He wanted to invite Missy. And of course," he added, "parents, guardians are always welcome."

"Thanks," Ellen said. "That sounds really nice. Missy loves putt-putt."

She and Jerry smiled at each other. When she glanced at Richard, he wasn't smiling. His expression was thoughtful as he glanced from her to Jerry.

Could it be possible?

Her heartbeat speeded up.

No. Richard couldn't be jealous.

&

During the rest of the week and into the next, Ellen had little time to either think of Richard or see him. Everyone worked frantically making sure all was ready for the dedication on

Friday. Besides that was the usual work of staff meetings, a couple of small conferences that came and went, new bookings, and the never-ending telephone and e-mail messages.

Along with the work came some volunteers, and Ellen began to understand why she'd heard over and over that Ridgeway couldn't do without them. An older couple, who had worked with MaryJo and Richard for a couple of summers, returned, and Ellen found them invaluable, not only in working, but in knowing what to do when she was uncertain.

Ellen liked dressing nicely every day instead of wearing jeans or slacks and her hair in a ponytail as she had at Little Tykes. For the dedication, she bought a new white summer suit to wear with a black shell and adorable black and white speckled high heels. She even put her hair back in a twist to give herself a more mature look. She liked feeling like a woman, involved in things, instead of a college-aged dropout.

She didn't know if Richard was really taken aback or if he were just kidding like that. But he looked and sounded serious when he came to work and said, "Everybody's going to be looking at you instead of the hotel. You look beautiful." His smile touched her heart.

"You look nice too," she said. His suit looked more formal than what he wore in the office, and his tie looked like silk against his white shirt. He always looked good to her. She suspected she thought of him too often, but she was so grateful for his giving her this job that was changing her life. She tried to remember that is was God who made all things possible, and she thanked Him.

At ten o'clock, Richard said she might want to go on to the hotel and be ready if people came earlier than ten-thirty, the time printed on the invitation. She already knew what kind of guests to expect. All the staff were invited, along with people who had some connection with Ridgeway, like local officials and pastors, including Ken and his girlfriend. Even Heather had been invited. They assumed that was because of her writing the article about the preschool.

Heather was in Ellen's first group of eight people that she led through the hotel. She felt even more at ease after the first tour. Like other staffers serving as tour guides, she led her group to a refreshment table, then took several more groups on the tour until time for the dedication service.

Following the welcome by the general manager, a woman gave a testimony about the meaning, purpose, and spiritual success of the center. The president of Christian resources gave the dedication message. That was followed by a solo, "Find Us Faithful," sung by the summer camps director. A final prayer was offered, then the guests were dismissed for lunch.

Since Ellen wore a name tag identifying her as a tour guide, several people stopped her to ask questions about the building or to express their feelings about the center—all favorable.

She was among the last to enter the dining room, and the elegance and beauty of it almost took her breath away. She'd seen the room, but not when it was decorated. Tables were set with gleaming dishes on white squares of cloth over maroon table coverings. Tall cloth napkins stood by each plate near glasses of tea and water. In the center of each table was an arrangement of multi-colored flowers. Tables sat on the same brown, beige, and maroon carpet. The brown-and-gold patterned, high-backed, padded chairs blended with the earth colors, and the gold drapes with their looped valances lent an elegant aura.

Then Ellen spied Heather, standing and waving. She'd saved her a seat at a table with some of the staff. Heather sat next to an older volunteer couple. Ellen's seat was next to Helen and Joe, a couple who had worked at Ridgeway after retirement. Across the way sat Jerry by an empty seat. Ellen thought she knew who would sit next to Jerry, and she was right. Richard soon came and occupied the seat.

Ellen was grateful Heather had come. Her friend could distract her from looking across into Richard's eyes. Ellen and the others talked about the elegant dessert at each place. Each dessert plate held a round pastry, filled with vanilla pudding,

and seated on red raspberry sauce. Pastry sprinkled with pow-
dered sugar formed wings, while another piece of curved pastry formed the long graceful neck of a swan. A small purple
lily adorned each plate.

After the invocation, a young man came to the table and
introduced himself as Tony, the server for the table. He
looked elegant in his white shirt, maroon vest, black tie, and
black pants. He served the table with finesse. From the apple-
nut-greens salad on a vinaigrette base to the Chicken Oscar
plate that included steamed shredded carrots, broccoli, and a
flower of toasted mashed potatoes, everything looked and
tasted marvelous. The hot rolls were light and flaky.

Joe, a former pilot spoke up. "Helen and I met at the center
in the dining room where we worked when we were college
students."

Helen, a lovely lady with a wonderful personality added,
"We shared our first kiss here."

That began talk about how many people had met at the
center and married.

"We have prayer brigade now," Jerry said.

Heather questioned that. "That wasn't here when I worked
here."

Richard explained. "No, it's been in effect a couple of years.
We built the new prayer garden, then discovered some of the
college students went there late at night when they were supposed to be in their rooms—and they didn't go for prayer. So
the prayer brigade sneaks up there, taking their big water
guns, and douses any unauthorized visitors good."

They all laughed. "But wait 'til you hear this," Jerry said.
"This old man came stomping into the general manager's
office one morning, telling his story. He and his wife had
been sprayed with water while they were on their knees praying. The brigade assumed it was young people. In the dark,
they couldn't tell."

Ellen loved the stories. She hadn't seriously thought about
meeting someone at Ridgeway and sharing a kiss with him,

but the idea certainly held appeal. Rather than yield to the temptation of looking into Richard's eyes, she shared glances and laughs with Heather.

She reminded herself that Richard seemed to like her, but he'd given no indication their relationship might be anything more than that of employer-employee and perhaps friends. Then with a sinking feeling in her stomach, she remembered all this was going to end in a week.

※

The workload had doubled after public schools let out for the school year and the summer programs began. Summer staff, mainly college students, inundated the campus. Lodges were filled to capacity with conferees.

Three weeks had passed since Tyler's birth.

On Friday, every time the phone rang, someone opened her office door, or Richard stepped into her office, Ellen expected to hear that this would be her last day—that MaryJo would return on Monday.

Perhaps she'd still be needed. How could MaryJo keep up with all the work after just having a baby?

The nearer to closing time the hands on the clock moved, the more fidgety Ellen became. She reprimanded herself when the thought occurred to her that maybe MaryJo wasn't able to return to work just yet. Ellen didn't want to go job-hunting again. In a way, it would have been best not to have worked here at all than have to leave—

The door opened. MaryJo came in with little Tyler in her arms. All thought of herself vanished as Ellen looked upon the faces of that precious baby and his radiant mom.

After the ooohs and aaahs and catching up on what had been going on in their lives, Ellen called Richard on the intercom. "MaryJo and Tyler are here to see you, Richard."

"Be right there."

Ellen detected the most wistful look in Richard's eyes, although he refused to hold the baby. But he made weird clucking sounds at the baby, who apparently found that delightful. Tyler resembled his mother, with his animated face and dark eyes. He cooed, gurgled, and slobbered, to everyone's delight. Especially MaryJo's.

She suddenly became serious. "I need to talk to you Richard."

"You want to come in the office?"

"I don't mind if Ellen hears me. She will have to know anyway."

Know? Of course. She wants her job back.

"Could I hold Tyler?" Ellen asked. Maybe MaryJo could talk more freely if Ellen held the baby.

"Oh, sure." She put the baby in Ellen's arms. That felt so wonderful. Ellen would love to have a baby of her own someday.

"It's this, Richard. And I hope you're not going to hate me," MaryJo began.

"No more than usual, I'm sure," he said and looked at her like he wanted her to respond to his jesting.

She did, with a grin and sideways glance at Ellen. She looked at Richard again, took a deep breath, and plunged in. "I can't come back to work."

He stared at her with a blank expression.

"There's just no way I can leave this baby." She gestured toward Tyler. "Now tell me, could you do that?"

He shrugged. "Um, well. Somebody has to pay the bills."

"Ben has a job. He can pay the bills. We figured up how much money we can save by having only one car and my not having to wear nice clothes every day. I can plan meals instead of throwing stuff together or getting fast food."

Richard surrendered. "I understand."

"Besides," she continued, as if he hadn't really understood, "if you bring a child into this world, then aren't you responsible for taking care of him?"

"I agree with you one hundred percent," he said.

MaryJo looked at Ellen with an apologetic expression. "Oh, I don't mean they're not supposed to go to preschool or a good day care when they get a little age on them. That's good for them too—learn things, associate with other children. But this is a baby!"

"You're kidding," Richard said. "Let me take another look."

He walked over to Ellen and Tyler, then faced MaryJo again. "I think you may be right."

"Oh, Richard." She lightly slapped his arm.

"Seriously, MaryJo," he said. "I can't fault you for this decision. I think you're right, and I respect you for it. But you're sure?"

"I am. I'll miss everybody, but I know this is right. I can't leave my baby, not even with my mom."

She reached out to Richard and they hugged—something Ellen had wanted to do a couple of times. Well, maybe more than a couple.

MaryJo stepped back with tears in her eyes. "You're a good man, Richard. I've loved working with you."

After MaryJo and Tyler left, Richard stood in Ellen's office for a moment. Would he ask her to make this temporary job a permanent one?

After a long moment, he spoke. "Ellen," he said. "Are you planning to return to college in the fall?"

❧

After Missy went to bed and a commercial came on, Ellen talked to her dad. Just as she feared, her elation was squelched when she told him that Richard had asked her to stay on. And she had agreed.

"Just for the summer?"

"No, Dad. Permanently. As long as I want to stay or as long as he wants me to."

She knew when he switched off the TV, she was about to get a lecture.

"So this means no college. No career. No goals for the future except working for that man. This is what you want to do for the rest of your life? When you could go anywhere in the world and prepare for any career? You'd rather stay with that man you claim is only your boss."

Ellen moved to the edge of the couch and turned to face him more directly. "Dad, how many times do I have to say this? I can't go off somewhere and prepare for a career as if Missy doesn't exist. She does exist. My responsibility is right here. My first priority is Missy."

"You're wrong." He spoke forcefully. Ellen blinked as if he'd struck her. "Missy is not your responsibility. She's mine."

This was not the man she'd known all her life. Was he jealous of her taking over with Missy? Did he want to be the little girl's sole support and caregiver? "Dad, I don't understand."

"Ellen, you've been forced into the mother role. For the past two years, I've let you take over all the responsibilities."

"I wanted it, Dad. She is my sister."

This seemed the perfect time for Ellen to say what she'd wanted to say for a long time. She reached over and enclosed his hand in hers. "Dad, let me adopt her."

"Ellen. She needs young parents."

"I'm young," she reminded him.

"But," he added, "you're single."

"I'll marry," Ellen said, knowing the only real prospect she had was hope. "Someday."

"I hope so, Ellen. But then what? You expect your husband to move in here? Can I turn over my daughter to some man I don't even know? Maybe your husband wouldn't want a ready-made family."

Ellen spoke quickly. "Then I wouldn't want him."

"Ah, Ellen. It's not that easy. Not when you find someone who makes your blood run fast. I felt that every time I looked at your mother."

"Now, Dad. I've heard you two argue, or as you called it, disagree."

"Well, like I said." He grinned with a twinkle in his eye. "She could make my blood boil."

They shared a laugh. For a moment, "Dad before Mom died" surfaced.

Then he became reminiscent. "But it was never dull. We loved each other. Respected each other. Liked each other."

Sadness clouded his face. "Ellen. Everything looked different when your mother was alive. I just don't have the energy to be a full-time dad again without Mary." He took a long breath. "I've even mentioned this to Daisy."

"Daisy?" Ellen moved her hands away, and her dad's hand lay limply on his pants leg. She wasn't sure where this was going. "Are. . .you thinking of her. . .taking care of Missy full time?"

He grimaced as though his thoughts were painful. "I've considered all possibilities, Ellen. But she's close to my age. After you raise little ones and they grow up, you think, 'Been there, done that.' Sounds terrible, doesn't it?"

"No, Dad. It sounds real. Is that what's been eating at you?"

He nodded. "What do we do when you marry? How do we divide that child?"

The answer seemed perfectly clear to Ellen. "Let me adopt her. I'll be her mom. You'll still be her Pa-Pa."

He stood and blinked away the emotion she knew he was trying hard to conceal. She'd seen her dad cry no more than a couple of times in her life. He looked close to it now. "That sounds like the perfect solution, Ellen. But my conscience won't let me allow that without considering other possibilities. You'll marry one of these days. If you adopt Missy, what kind of man would be her dad?"

How ridiculous could he get? "Dad, what kind of man do you think I'd marry?"

"The right kind, I hope. But Ellen, you don't even have any prospects, do you?"

How could she answer such a thing? Prospects? "I have no one asking to marry me, if that's what you mean."

"Exactly. Frankly, I would need to approve any man I would turn my daughter over to." He shook his head as if this were a hopeless situation. She could hardly believe what he said next. "I talked to Leanne today."

"You called her?"

"I asked her to visit. I want her to see Missy."

That left Ellen speechless.

"Don't look so shocked, Ellen. I've been telling you. You're not Missy's mom. Before it's too late, I need to consider what Mary and I discussed when we took Missy in as a baby. Maybe she and her birth mom need each other now."

Ellen didn't think anything could upset her more than being without her mother. But her dad's words absolutely floored her.

"Dad, you can't be serious. You can't uproot Missy from the only home she's ever known."

"Ellen, this breaks my heart. But I'm trying to put that child's needs ahead of my own. And, Honey, you're my child too. I have to do what I think is best for you."

Ellen saw the heartache in his eyes. She also saw his resoluteness.

He gave Ellen a long, sad look. Then with a crumpled face he turned and walked from the room. That's how it was. He never argued or discussed issues for long when disagreements arose. He stated his opinion and as far as he was concerned, that meant his opinion was written in stone.

He was dead serious.

thirteen

All weekend, Ellen functioned like she had after she was told her mom died. The news hadn't seemed real. Not even when all the funeral plans were being made or when she was sitting at the service. She'd been fine.

Several days after the funeral, however, the reality of Ellen's loss had overwhelmed her. She'd turned up the music on the radio and gone into the shower. Her wails of "No, no, no" accompanied the tears that washed her face. After that, she'd cried with Heather and alone, several times.

Now, facing the possible loss of Missy, she kept telling herself this was no situation for grief. Her dad wouldn't take Missy from her. He wouldn't do it to Missy.

She understood her dad's reasoning. From his point of view, it sounded right. Ellen had to ask herself if she wanted Missy for her own sake. Was Missy filling the void left by her mom's death? Was she being selfish, wanting Missy? Was Leanne the best one for Missy?

Dad was right too about something being done as soon as possible, if it were to be done. Leanne was Missy's birth mother.

Ellen decided to simply pray harder for her Dad to come to his senses. He would. He wanted her to revert to being a young, single college girl with career or marriage on her mind. She couldn't turn back time. She'd have to convince him of that. Maybe enlist Daisy, Heather, the pastor—anybody she could think of—to get through to him.

At work on Monday, Ellen managed to control her emotions until near closing time. But she had to answer the question of why she had told Richard she would stay on with this job. Had her decision been based on being near Missy? Or had it been based on the possibility of being near Richard Williams?

She had agreed for both reasons, she told herself. But the floodgates opened, and the liquid heartache spilled out.

The phone rang while she was in the bathroom trying to repair her face. She let the answering machine pick up. When she came out, the door between her office and Richard's was open. He must have wondered where she had gone. Whenever she left the office, she'd tell him where she was going, or simply say, "If you don't need me, I'll be back in a jif," and he'd acknowledge that, usually with an "Okay."

Their eyes met. She'd just stopped crying. Then it started again. She hurried to her desk and pulled out another tissue and began to swipe at the tears.

"Ellen?" He came and stood in the doorway.

"I'm fine. Just. . .emotional. I'm. . .sorry."

"Sorry," he said in a teasing voice. "You're sorry you agreed to keep this job?"

She laughed lightly at his attempt at joking, but the water-works wouldn't turn off. She owed him some kind of explanation for crying. She walked past her desk and came to stand near him. "It's my family situation. Dad thinks I will get married and wonders what will happen to Missy then. I want to adopt her. I don't think he's going to let me."

He reached out and held her arm. "Ellen, I know how much you and Missy mean to each other. I think she belongs with you." His expression was pained. "But then, I'm partial."

Ellen gazed at him. Partial? He had special feelings for them? For her?

Their gaze held. She felt the strength of his hand on her arm. Was that a special caring in his eyes? Maybe it was a reflection of her own longing—not his. Her own fantasies—not his. But she knew he was a caring man.

He let go of her arm, an action she took as meaning she'd invaded his space.

"I'm sorry. I shouldn't have burdened you with my problems. I'm okay." She turned, but not before her tears began to bathe her face. Oh, how she hated being such an emotional wreck.

Before she reached her desk, he turned her to face him. He placed his hands on her shoulders. He was so close and spoke softly. "You're not okay. If I have any authority at all around here, you'll come into my office and talk to me."

Authority had nothing to do with it. She wanted to respond to his caring attitude. And she owed him some kind of explanation for falling apart on the job. She sniffed. "I have to pick up Missy."

"Can someone else do that?"

She nodded. There were plenty of people to do that. Her dad. Daisy. Heather if she was home. All her friends, neighbors, and church members were eager to help. Her dad could hire two-dozen nannies. Who needed Ellen?

"You don't want her to see you like this, do you?"

She shook her head.

"It's almost closing time. Let's go up to my house and talk. Can I call someone for you?"

"I will."

He moved his hands away, but she still felt the warmth of them, along with the caring look in his eyes. She was glad when Daisy answered instead of her dad. She'd break down again if she had to speak to him just now.

Daisy said she or Jon would pick up Missy.

"I'm going to be here for awhile, Daisy. Don't wait supper on me."

"Okay, Honey. Don't worry about anything here."

"Thanks. I won't. Bye."

She hung up. No, she didn't need to worry about anything at home. They'd manage fine without her.

❧

"Working late, huh?" Jon said to Daisy when she told him either he or she needed to pick up Missy.

Daisy shrugged a shoulder. "She didn't say 'working,' Jon."

He grinned. "Maybe things are looking up."

"Now, Jon. . ."

He frowned. "Don't contradict me, Woman. Maybe she's coming around to my way of thinking. I know she believes she has to raise Missy. I know how she feels. But I have to try and push her away from that, so she can live her own life without feeling guilty about it. This has to be my doing. You understand?"

"I understand what you're saying, Jon. But I'm not sure if you're right. If she has to give up Missy, it will break her heart."

"Yes, I know. But people can get over a broken heart if they have the right person to help them. You know what I mean?"

"Not exactly, Jon. You'll have to spell it out for me."

He turned to walk away, grumbling, "Obviously, I'm not a very good speller."

❧

Ellen wanted to drive her own car farther up the mountain to Richard's house rather than have him drive her back down to the center. She arrived before he did and sat in the car on the concrete drive near the front of his house. The driveway was bordered by a rock wall about four feet high, back from which grew rhododendron that had to be several years old. They mingled with a forest of maple, oak, and dogwood trees. He had no flowerbeds, but azalea bushes that had already lost their blossoms edged the house. High on the deck was one splotch of bright color—a hanging basket laden with multi-colored petunias.

She got out when Richard drove up.

"Supper," he said, climbing out of his car. "Straight from the Ridgeway kitchen."

So that's what had taken him so long. He held two carry-out boxes. She followed him up to the deck at the second level. He held the boxes out to her. "If you'll take these out back, I'll go through the house and get silverware and some-thing to drink."

Ellen knew the deck wrapped completely around the chalet. It would be nice sitting on the deck looking out on the fantastic view. She hadn't paid much attention, however, until she reached the back and realized the sky was overcast. The pool water lay still, reflecting the gray of the clouds that obscured the view of the mountains.

They ate, talked about such trivial things as the hot sultry day, and were thankful for a light breeze making the humidity bearable. Richard spoke of the float that Ridgeway was making under Jerry's supervision for the upcoming Fourth of July parade.

Talking to Richard was easy. He was a friend.

As Ellen finished the spice cake, she realized her tears had dried completely. Her fears had been put at the back of her mind. She recalled her dad saying it wouldn't be easy giving up someone she cared about if he didn't want a ready-made family. For a moment, she understood what he meant.

But she wasn't faced with such a choice.

Richard hadn't indicated an interest in anything beyond friendship. And if he were to do so, she didn't think that she would have to worry about his attitude toward Missy. Richard liked children.

Suppose, just suppose, her dad did something unthinkable and gave Missy back to Leanne. Although it would break her heart, she could imagine leaning on Richard, as she had leaned on Heather after the loss of her mother.

All her thoughts returned to the issue at hand, however, after Richard threw away their boxes and brought out coffee for them both. They turned their chairs toward the view, still obscured.

"I shouldn't burden you," she said.

"No burden," he said. "Even if all I can do is listen, I'm willing."

That's what she'd come here for, wasn't it? What else? She fought back the answer. "Dad is Missy's legal parent. He says my raising Missy is unfair to me because I should get my education, get married, have children of my own." She sighed. "If he does something foolish like trying to give her back to Leanne, her birth mother, I'd want to take it to court."

Even as she said it, she faced the absurdity of that. "But how could I fight my own dad? How could I even hope to win a court case against Missy's legal dad and her birth mother?"

Observing the thoughtful expression on his face, Ellen waited for his response. Finally, he spoke in a low tone, as if to himself. "Ellen, how could Leanne give up her own daughter?"

She told him about Leanne's situation. "She was only fourteen when she became pregnant. Her mom was divorced, had a job, and couldn't care for the baby. Mom and Dad agreed to keep Missy for awhile to make sure she and her mom were making the right decision. After a year, they decided they still couldn't care properly for Missy."

"Ellen," he said. "Couldn't your dad be doing the same thing? Making a sacrifice for the good of both his children?"

That's not what she wanted to hear. "It's not right," she protested. She stood, set her cup on the table, then walked over and stood with her back against a post that ran from the railing to the roof over the deck.

"Ellen, I'm not saying it's right. I'm just trying to make you see his point of view. This sounds to me like his decision is based on love for Missy and on what he thinks is best for you."

"He's wrong. Oh, Richard, he is so wrong." Then the moisture fell, not from the clouds, but from her eyes.

Richard jumped up. "Ellen, I'm not saying he's right. I'm just saying understand him so you can talk to him."

She felt his hands on her shoulders. Saw the concern in his blurry countenance, heard it in his voice. "I know you love that child like she's your own. She loves you." His voice became a whisper, and he softly spoke her name. "Ellen."

Richard was holding her. Consoling her. Wiping away her tears.

"If my dad makes me lose Missy, then I'll be losing my dad too. Oh, this is so hard." The tears started again.

"I know, Ellen. I know."

She felt his heartbeat. Or was it her own?

She looked up at him. His words didn't sound like a trite,

repeated phrase. His face was so close. His expression so full of caring. He really seemed to know. "You've lost someone, haven't you, Richard?"

His arms around her stiffened. Finally he laughed, without humor. "We're discussing you tonight, Ellen. Not me."

Would they ever discuss him? Or was he so protective of his inner self that one dared not intrude?

Yes, the lion in him was showing again.

&

Richard realized his wayward hand had caressed Ellen's back as he held her. Even now, as she looked up at him with questioning eyes, her face was so close to his, lifted to his own—how easy it would be. . .how easy. . .

He became aware of himself as a man holding a woman, a soft, warm, appealing woman. For an instant, the moment had become something other than a boss consoling his employee, a man consoling a woman. He wanted to give in to the growing feelings in his heart and pursue a relationship with her. But that included revealing things that he'd tried to put behind him. How much did a person have to reveal about the past?

Acceptance had not come easy for him. He'd given that situation from his past to God but kept taking it back. He'd lost respect for himself. He didn't want to lose Ellen's respect.

He moved back, lest she detect the increase in his heart rate. *Get hold of yourself, Richard. You know better than to let this happen.*

Had Ellen wondered about his hasty retreat? She turned and held onto the railing. No, her mind wasn't on him at all. His shouldn't have been on her. He sat in his chair, forcing his thoughts back to the issue at hand.

Richard believed if he had been married, had a child, and the child's mom died, he would not even consider giving up the child. Yet if he were a grandfather and the situation was like Jon Jonsen's, he might think like him. Mr. Jonsen's attitude seemed totally unselfish. As did the action of Missy's birth mother when she was fourteen.

But Richard also knew he would want his birth child. He believed that would be best—whether the child came to him at age four or fourteen.

He also agreed that the ideal for Missy or any child was two loving parents. But this was not an ideal world. And after seeing Ellen's grief at the prospect of losing Missy, he could honestly say, "Ellen, I believe you and Missy love each other as much as any parent and child could."

She faced him then, smiled through her tears, and managed a weak, "Thank you for saying that."

He almost said that if God wanted her and Missy to be together, then they would. But he couldn't say that with complete confidence. Sometimes people got themselves into situations contrary to the will of God. They had to live with the consequences. Everything was not the way God preferred it.

"We'll pray, Ellen. For God's will in this situation." That was the best he could do.

She nodded. "Somehow, I have to convince Dad that Missy and I belong together."

Yes, he thought. *But how?*

fourteen

"Ellen asked me if I'd ever lost anyone," Richard said to Jerry a few days later at lunch in the cafeteria. "I couldn't tell her, Jerry. I've never told anyone but you. I think I would have exploded if I hadn't had you to talk to. I couldn't even do that until after you lost Amy."

"I have a book that might help you, Richard. A book on grieving."

"Grieving? Jerry, why a book on grieving? I think Ellen is handling her mother's death quite well. She understands her emotional fragility. Remembering at odd times. She's talked about that."

Jerry was nodding. "Yes, Richard. She's open and honest about her feelings. About losing her mother and now about possibly losing Missy. But this book is not for her, Richard. It's for you."

"I'm not grieving."

Jerry was relentless. "I think you are."

Richard scoffed. "Jerry, you can't grieve over someone who's never been yours."

"Sure you can. People can grieve over losing a job, failing a test, breaking a leg, anything. And your situation is bigger than that." Jerry's eyes misted over. "Amy had a miscarriage before Jacob. You've seen how MaryJo and Ben acted when they were expecting. Well, Amy and I were just as excited. And when she miscarried, we grieved. I don't know how to measure grief, but it was just as real as when I lost Amy. Will you read the book? Consider what I'm saying."

Richard had known it for years, but it was impressed upon him again that Jerry was more than a friend. He was Richard's only confidant. They'd helped each other reason through and pray through some of life's most difficult situations, both bitter and sweet.

Richard promised to take a look at the book.

❧

The next day, the door was open between Richard's and Ellen's offices when Jerry walked in with a book in his hand, the title in plain view while he talked with Ellen.

"Here's the book I mentioned," Jerry said, when Richard walked in.

"Thanks." Richard quickly changed the subject, lest Ellen ask about the book. "How's the float coming along?"

"We're still working on it," Jerry said. "That's one reason I stopped by. You two come down and see. It's almost finished."

"It better be," Richard quipped. "Tomorrow's the Fourth." He looked over and winked at Ellen.

Ellen's expression questioned Richard, who grinned and then looked at Jerry. "You go on. We'll be there shortly."

After Jerry left, Richard went into his office and put the book in a desk drawer. He returned to Ellen's office and pushed the buttons that switched the phone to the answering machine. Then he took her hand in his. "Come on. Break time."

She rose, laughing with him. He let go of her hand, and they walked to the site of the center's Fourth of July float that would be driven in the downtown parade. Richard spied Jerry and some of the staff and summer college students working on the float.

Jerry noticed the new arrivals just then and called out, "Ellen, you know the preschool and day-care children will ride on the float, don't you?"

Ellen nodded. "Missy is so excited about it. Hey, let me do something. At least one thing."

"Sure, come on over. You too, Richard."

They went over. Jerry had each of them screw in one of the battery-operated candles that would surround the float. "Now you can say you helped."

Aware of his standing there, laughing and associating with

Ellen and Jerry, two people so valuable to him in many ways, Richard felt blessed. Soon, however, he had to say, "Ellen, we'd better get back to work."

Walking back to the office on a beautiful summer day, Richard was aware of the bright sunshine that turned Ellen's hair to a light golden brown. She often looked at him, her cheek dimpling, in a way that made him think she thought him special.

Sometimes around her, he felt as mature as a high school kid. He thought of the late evening when the singles' group had come to his house and gone swimming. Jerry had commented, "No disrespect intended, but she's easy on the eyes."

"Who?" Richard pretended innocence.

"Your administrative assistant."

Richard knew how she looked. It was common knowledge that men were attracted to women. He saw her five days a week at work. He liked the way she looked. He'd learned how to handle physical attraction and not be disrespectful by harboring lustful thoughts.

But what he had a problem with was her more impressive qualities. Those were the thoughts that lingered. How could one pray, "God, help me not have such beautiful thoughts about this person?"

To make it worse, he thought he saw in her eyes the willingness to go beyond friendship.

What was he going to do about those thoughts before they turned into an irrevocable condition of the heart? She had brought something wonderful into his life by her commitment to the Lord and to her little sister. She had confided in him. She apparently looked to him as a mature man with possible answers to some of life's problems.

He was pretty good at that—except when it came to his own problems.

But he wanted to help her.

Then he had an idea that might help him put an end to his growing feelings for her and help several people at the same time. It could also influence Ellen's dad to reconsider doing anything too hastily.

He'd prayed about all aspects of the situation—within the office and out. Then he recalled a story about a person who had asked a pastor, "Why doesn't God do something about the poverty in the world?"

The pastor had replied, "That's what he put you here for."

Okay, then, perhaps it was time for Richard Williams to put feet to his prayers. Right after the Fourth, he would do. . . something.

๛

Ellen and Heather stood on the sidewalk downtown and watched the parade go by. There wasn't much to it compared with what the TV showed. But each year it grew more patriotic. Just about everybody waved a flag. Onlookers weren't just observers anymore, but participants.

"Oh, I need to talk to Patsy. Come on." Heather began walking farther down the sidewalk.

Ellen had dreaded it, but she knew it was inevitable that she and Patsy would run into each other at some point. Might as well get the encounter over with.

Patsy looked startled when Heather walked up beside her and said, "Hi, Mrs. Hatcher."

She glanced over. "Good afternoon, Heather. Hello, Ellen."

Ellen could think no other response but, "Hello," and a brief smile that she hoped didn't look fake. Much as she might have found it difficult to believe at the time, she had become glad that Patsy had fired her. That action had led to so much good for both Ellen and Missy. Ellen kept her eyes fixed on the floats.

"I believe the parade's a little bigger this year," Patsy said.

"I don't think I saw it last year," Heather replied. "I thought I might see you here. I wanted to tell you I got an E-mail this morning from the magazine. The editor loves the article about Little Tykes. I'll send you half the money when I get the check."

"No, no." Patsy shook her head. "You wrote an excellent article that will be wonderful publicity for the school. You keep the money. You've earned it. I don't need it."

"Thank you," Heather said.

Ellen was reminded that Patsy was a good person. She would continue to pray for her.

"Oh, there's Missy." Heather waved with her arm above her head.

Missy waved and shouted. "Hi, Mommy! Hi, Heather! Hi, Mrs. Hatcher!" Her voice carried over the camp director singing, "My Country, 'Tis of Thee," and Richard playing the drums for accompaniment.

The float's skirt was white with red hearts and gold stars. Printed in blue letters were the words, "JESUS IS THE LIGHT OF THE WORLD." The battery-operated candles glowed around the edge of the floor of the float. The children waved Christian flags.

Ellen pretended to not hear Heather pointing out that the drummer was Ellen's new boss and Patsy's response that she was glad things were working out well for Ellen and Missy.

"Oh, your float looks great," Heather said to Patsy as the Little Tykes float began to move by.

Ellen agreed the float looked beautiful, decorated with numerous cartoon characters. Little Tykes Preschool children and workers sat on it. Ellen and Missy had been with them last year. Missy, a year younger then, had sat close to Ellen, perhaps for a sense of security. This year, the brave little girl expressed her independence without Ellen right beside her.

As soon as the last float passed by, Patsy said good-bye to Heather and Ellen. "I feel a chill. I think I'll go on. I don't want to get caught in all the traffic. Have a good day."

"You too," Ellen and Heather replied.

Ellen's gaze followed Patsy, walking swiftly along Main Street to the parking lot that belonged to a friend of hers who was a shop owner and always let Patsy park there. Ellen looked at the big sign at the bank that gave the temperature of eighty-seven degrees. Patsy felt a chill? Maybe it was just nerves. Ellen had felt a little uncomfortable herself when she and Heather first walked up to Patsy.

"Oh, no," Ellen exclaimed suddenly, seeing Patsy falling. The woman tried to brace herself. Her hands seemed to give way, and her head stuck the concrete sidewalk.

"Mrs. Hatcher." Heather was one of the first to reach Patsy.

Almost immediately, an EMT was at the injured woman's side. Soon an ambulance arrived.

Patsy was saying, "I'm all right. I'm all right."

The EMT said, "Ma'am, you'll be fine, but it looks like you have a broken arm. You have anyone who can ride with you?"

Nobody spoke, including Patsy. Ellen knew the woman had no relatives in the area. Her dad had already planned to pick up Missy after the parade. "Can I ride with you?" Ellen asked.

On the stretcher, Patsy's eyes squeezed shut, as if she were in pain. Heather rode in back with Patsy, and Ellen rode in front with the driver, who sounded the siren as the ambulance headed for the hospital in Asheville.

Later, they learned that Patsy had a broken arm. The doctors wanted to keep her overnight for observation since she had also suffered a head injury.

Ellen had already called Daisy so that she might either come and get her and Heather or watch Missy while her dad came.

"I'll stay in touch with the hospital," Heather said later on the way home. "I'll keep you informed about Patsy."

❧

The next morning at work, Ellen told Richard about Patsy.

"You're remarkable, Ellen," he said. "She's the one who fired you, isn't she?"

Ellen smiled, not holding back her joy. "That turned out to be a great blessing."

"Good," he said, but the way he avoided her gaze by looking down at the floor made her wonder if she were too transparent. Then he looked up and asked, "Are you busy tomorrow night?"

If she hadn't been sitting in the chair behind her desk, Ellen thought she would have fallen. Was he asking her for a date? She suddenly realized she hadn't dated in two years.

"Could you be at the Eclectic at six o'clock?"

The Eclectic! That was one of the two nicer places in Ridgeway. Expensive too.

"Yes," she said, all the while thinking she'd have little more than an hour after work to get ready for what could be one of the most important days of her life.

"I've asked Jerry if he will talk to you. I think he could help you with this problem with your dad, since Jerry's a single parent. He's also lost his wife, and you might find it helpful if he talks to your dad."

Ellen stared at a letter on her desk while nodding slightly, avoiding Richard's eyes. He wasn't asking her for a date. He was trying to help her with a bigger problem. She had to get her mind back on track. It had wandered way too far.

She wanted to say that she could talk to Jerry anywhere. Why the Eclectic? She felt like shouting, "Is it Dutch treat?"

Oh dear. Ellen, control yourself. He's trying to help you with the most important matter in your life. Appreciate it. "Why talk there?" she managed to say.

"The atmosphere," Richard said. "And I would like to treat my friend and my employee to a nice dinner. The reservation is in my name. You know how to get there?"

"Yes, I've eaten there." She didn't add, "Once."

"Great." He turned and strode back into his office. She thought his face had flushed. Had he known she'd assumed he was asking her for a date when he'd asked if she were busy?

Well, he couldn't really know her thoughts.

She'd committed to this "date" before she knew the circumstances. How could she bow out gracefully?

Especially when Richard was trying to be a friend.

❧

"Maybe Richard is going to show up," Heather said that evening, rummaging through Ellen's closet for the right outfit.

"I don't know. I wasn't about to ask. Even if he does, I'm going to feel. . .funny."

"Funny? With two handsome men? Well, give me one."

"Oh, go with me!"

Heather shook her head. "No, I'll just wait for your leftovers."

Ellen shook her head and tried to be jolly. They decided she should wear her beige silk dress, gold earrings, and heels. Not too dressy, but not as conservative as what she wore in the office.

Just in case Richard showed up.

She warned herself to stop thinking like that. Again, this was not a date. It was simply a helpful gesture from her boss.

æ

Ellen sat at the table in the Eclectic, looking at the card on the golden disk in front of her that sat on a lace tablecloth. She opened it and read:

In appreciation for my most efficient administrative assistant.
Richard

Hey! And it wasn't even officially Administrative Assistant Appreciation Day.

Maybe Richard did intend to join them. He might have thought it would look strange, picking her up as if this were a date, then meeting Jerry.

Smiling, she closed the card, tucked it away in her purse, and looked around at the European decor. The flicker of candlelight from each table emitted a warm glow. A classical pianist accompanied a young woman who stood back in the shadows, softly singing love songs. How could anyone not succumb to such a romantic setting?

She held her breath when she realized the waitress was escorting a man toward her. Not Richard, but Jerry.

They spoke to each other, but he hesitated before sitting. Ellen returned Jerry's uncomfortable smile and refused to look at him again. She kept her attention fixed on the waitress.

In the unromantic silence, the waitress asked, "Would you like something to drink?"

"No!" they said in unison.

The waitress stepped back. "I'll bring your menus."

"Is Richard coming?" Ellen asked.

"I don't think he planned to, Ellen. He told me he would like for me to talk with you about your situation with your dad and Missy. He really thinks I might be able to help. But—" He cleared his throat. "I know how it looks with his having us meet here." He raised his hand. "Don't explode. It's kind of funny."

Ellen looked away. Real funny! She was dressed in a way she hoped would make Richard find her attractive, sitting across from Jerry who wore a knit shirt and casual slacks. No tie. But that's not what mattered.

"Oh, Ellen. I don't mean it's funny being with you. It's funny what Richard is doing. Oh, foot! Maybe it's not funny."

She looked at him then, and rather than cry, she laughed. Jerry plainly saw this as a setup. She had to blink away the moisture of anger, hurt, disappointment, confusion, frustration, embarrassment—every vile emotion one could have.

"Why would he try and be a matchmaker? Doesn't he think we could do this on our own if we wanted?"

He shrugged a shoulder. "Well, you gotta understand him."

Ellen nodded. "I think I'm understanding him loud and clear."

Jerry grimaced. "Well, Ellen. I suspect he wanted to take you out and got cold feet. He did tell me he thought we should talk about your situation. He also told me he'd made reservations here for six o'clock for my birthday, which is Sunday by the way, in case you want to get me a present. Kidding."

She smiled. So, the world was full of jokers! And this joke was on her. Foolish, foolish girl! "He doesn't strike me as one to have cold feet."

Jerry grew serious. "In the area of serious personal relations, he does."

That was hard to believe. "Why?"

He shook his head and smiled sadly. "Sorry, I can't betray a confidence."

Now that piqued her interest. "But there's something? I saw you give him that book on grief. Is he grieving over something or someone?" That might explain Richard's actions when she had asked if he had ever lost anyone. Was he dealing with something too difficult to discuss?

Jerry simply grimaced and looked around as the waitress came.

"Would you like to know what the special of the house is tonight?" she asked.

Jerry looked at Ellen, who wondered if she should say she'd rather just go. But he smiled and said, "Sure."

Ellen suspected it would be cooked goose.

fifteen

"Pan-fried trout. Herbed mashed potatoes. Steamed broccoli. House salad." The waitress handed them the menus and walked way.

"I'm sorry, Ellen," Jerry said.

"It's nice of Richard to do this—I guess," Ellen said.

Jerry took a deep breath, held it for quite a long moment, then exhaled. "I know how it looks, Ellen. And I don't know how to say this, without insulting you, but I didn't put him up to this. I haven't implied anything that might cause him to do this."

He seemed so sincere and uncomfortable, Ellen believed him. "Well, neither have I," she said. "I mean, I've said I thought you were a nice person. That's the extent of it. I mean I might have said, 'You're the greatest,' or something. That I liked you."

"And I admit I've said. . .let's see. . .what were the exact words?" He looked toward the darkened ceiling, then at her again. "That he was fortunate to have found you at the time MaryJo was leaving. He said you were very capable, efficient, and dedicated."

Jerry sighed and shook his head. "Confession time. I also said you were attractive." He spread his hands. "But believe me, I didn't mean a thing disrespectful." He gulped. "Maybe he took me wrong. However, why shouldn't two nice, attractive—whoa, you didn't say I was attractive though, did you?"

Ellen laughed. "I'll say it, Jerry. You're. . .there's nothing wrong with you."

"Okay." He laughed. "Why shouldn't two nice, attractive single people have dinner together?" He grinned. "Especially when it's paid for. Richard said this is on his credit card."

Ellen was grateful the room was dim. Maybe he couldn't see her cheeks, which she felt must surely be flaming. Not just with embarrassment, but with a sense of chagrin that anyone would do something like this to her.

"I believe you," she said. "I'm sorry to say this, but rumor has it that you're not interested in dating."

A sadness crossed his face. "That's true. It's not that I can't accept my wife's death. But I won't burden you with my life story."

"It would not be a burden, Jerry. I've had losses of my own. But, if this is too uncomfortable, we can leave."

He remained silent for what seemed an eternity, looking down at the round gold plate in front of him. Finally, he looked up. His eyes were warm. "I've known Richard for several years now. He's a confirmed bachelor, but he loves the idea of family. He means well. But I don't like surprise dates. I think he did it because he likes us both. He thought we'd hit it off." Jerry held his head. "Oh, man. I'm making a mess of this."

"No, no, you're not. I understand. Well, I don't exactly understand Richard's reasoning. But I understand what you mean." She leaned back. "Shall we go?"

He looked sheepish. "Pan-fried trout sounds really good to me. I'm a fisherman. Or rather I used to be. Too busy for that most of the time, with work and Jacob." He sighed heavily. "Maybe if we have a meal together we can get back to being comfortable with each other."

Ellen nodded. Pan-fried trout sounded good to her too, but she didn't want to give the impression she and Jerry had a lot in common. She opened the menu. Many of the entrees looked equally good. She chose the chicken cordon bleu.

They both ordered coffee to keep them busy while waiting.

"So," Ellen said, after the waitress took their menus. "You said you're a fisherman." She laughed lightly. "Or used to be."

By the time the waitress brought their coffee and wheeled over the house salad, on which both accepted fresh black pepper from a pepper mill, they were engrossed in conversation about the area streams and rivers liked by fishermen.

Jerry paused. "Shall we say grace?"

Ellen nodded.

They bowed their heads. Jerry thanked God for Richard's friendship, for the opportunity to make new friends, and for the food.

Ellen knew Jerry was attempting to put everything in perspective. At the "Amen," he opened his eyes and smiled, then continued the conversation where they had left off. "I like the river, but Jacob prefers the streams he can wade in and toss the line, whether or not he's catching any fish."

"I never took to fishing very much," Ellen admitted. "But Dad loves it, and so does Missy. He doesn't go much anymore either."

By the time the entrée arrived, she'd told Jerry about her mom's death, her dad's sadness and ongoing grief, and her concern about Missy.

"I know our ultimate purpose in life is to serve the Lord, but we have our human responsibilities. A man's identity is wrapped up in his job, Ellen. His reason for going to work every day is for his family, taking care of his wife. Amy was my reason for waking up in the morning, for going to work. I can teach Jacob about men's work—the trash, the yard, sports. But when it comes to the tenderness, the emotional side of things, I feel totally inadequate. I can understand how your dad feels. I would like to talk to him. He could likely be helpful to me."

At the end of the meal, they discussed dessert. "We don't want Richard to get off easy, do we?" Jerry asked.

Ellen laughed. "No way."

Each ordered blueberries flambeau and delighted in the waitress preparing the concoction at their table. They, and patrons near them, laughed when the contents of the pan flamed up right at their table.

"Ellen," Jerry said after a couple of bites. "Maybe we should give this a trial run and see what happens. Wouldn't want to hurt Richard's feelings, would we?

Yes, she would!

But that was anger and hurt thinking. That isn't what she wanted at all. Had anyone but Richard done this, she would think it clever. She blinked away the emotion. Her gaze met Jerry's.

"For Richard's sake," he said, with a knowing look in his eyes. "And yours."

She swallowed a big lump of ice cream and waited for the headache matching her heartache.

Looked like she and Jerry understood each other. And who knew what might come of it?

They even sat through another cup of coffee.

⁂

Ellen arrived home a little past nine o'clock. Missy was already in bed asleep.

Daisy and her dad were watching TV.

"Have a good time, Dear?" Daisy asked, rising from her chair.

Ellen could answer that truthfully. "I sure did. Jerry is a great guy."

"Jerry?" She gave Ellen a "what's going on" look. "I thought you were having dinner with Richard. Was it a double date?"

"No. Just me and Jerry."

Her dad even turned off the TV. "You sure you didn't go out with Richard? That boss of yours?"

"No, Dad." She raised her hand to her chest. "Did I say, 'Richard'? I had dinner with Jerry. You know, the one who had the birthday party that Missy and I went to. Oh, and he likes to fish."

"What kind? Deep sea?"

Ellen laughed. "No, Dad. The same kind you like—fishing the streams for rainbow trout."

Her dad pursed his lips and nodded. "He sounds okay so far."

"Don't leave on my account, Daisy," she said as Daisy walked toward the kitchen. "I'm beat. Going to bed."

"I need to go home and do that too," Daisy said. "Good night, Jon."

"Night." He switched off the TV and looked at Ellen. "I'm glad you had a good time, Honey."

She nodded, went over, and bent for his hug. She kissed him on the cheek and for a meaningful moment he held her arms. "I love you, Dad."

"I love you too."

Ellen went to her room, telling herself she hadn't lied about Richard and Jerry. One just didn't need to tell everybody, everything, every time.

It had been her own wishful thinking that Richard might be personally interested in her. Maybe he had been. But he was a confirmed bachelor. She knew he liked children, but maybe a thirty-five-year-old bachelor was like her dad had said, not interested in taking on a ready-made family.

Or maybe he just didn't like her. . .romantically.

During that night, Ellen cried. She reminded herself of what she'd felt when she'd heard of girls going back to guys who were no good for them or becoming weeping willows when they were jilted or returned to abusers saying something as foolish as, "But I love him."

Love!

She understood it now.

She knew she wouldn't stand for abuse, she wouldn't chase a guy who ran the other way, she wouldn't accept a man who wasn't good for her. But the other part—the feelings—she wasn't entirely in control of. Feelings and actions, she reminded herself, were two different things, and she was in control of her actions.

Should she quit her job if feelings got in the way? She'd seen old movies where secretaries stayed with their bosses for decades, pining away for them, giving their lives to someone they couldn't have.

She wouldn't be that way.

But she couldn't quit her job just now. Not with this situation with her dad about Missy.

She shouldn't quit anyway because Richard set her up with Jerry. He apparently thought he was honoring his employee and friend with a special dinner. Neat idea, huh? He must think a lot of her to set her up with his best friend. She'd have to thank him.

But at the moment, she would just cry him out of her system.

Thank you, God, that tomorrow is Saturday. I'll wear cucumber slices on my puffy eyes all weekend. ❧

"My pleasure," Richard said Monday morning after Ellen thanked him for the dinner at the Eclectic, but she seemed different. Friendly as ever, but somehow reserved.

Then Jerry stopped by, smiling from ear to ear. He walked into Richard's office, talking about what a great friend Richard was to think of a dinner, with a date no less, for his birthday. Very creative.

When he left Richard's office, Jerry kept the door open, and Richard watched him lean over Ellen's desk and talk to her, like Richard had done at times. On second glance, not exactly like he'd done. Richard hadn't leaned over quite that far, with quite that silly look on his face, and he didn't think Ellen had smiled up into his face like that.

Richard drew in a deep breath.

That was good, wasn't it? What he wanted, wasn't it?

What better thing could happen for two of the finest people he knew than to get together? This might help Ellen's dad think twice about not letting Ellen adopt Missy. If she and Jerry married, she'd be a mom to Jacob. It would be foolish not to let her be a mom to Missy.

Awhile passed before Richard realized Jerry had turned toward him. "Hey," he called, waving his hand in circles like people do when they imply you don't really see or hear them. "So long."

Richard forced a laugh and pointed to some papers on his desk and made circles at his head, meaning he had been deep in thought about his work. "See ya," Richard said.

Jerry and Ellen said final good-byes, then Jerry left.

Richard sat staring at his desk for a long moment before he got up and closed his office door.

❧

Quite often, Richard and Jerry ran into each other at lunchtime in the dining hall. Feeling restless, Richard decided not to wait until Ellen returned from lunch. Sometimes she had errands to run and was a little late. She'd be back soon. He went to the dining hall and filled his plate from the serving line and walked into the dining room, searching for someone he might sit with. He saw Jerry and Ellen.

Never before had he been reluctant to sit with friends or coworkers. But they seemed to be having such a good time, eating, talking, laughing. Yes, he'd been right. Those two hit it off. He'd done well, getting them together.

Just as Richard started to sit at another table, Jerry looked his way and motioned for him to come over. He shouldn't be reluctant. After all, Jerry was his best friend.

He sat.

"Uh oh," Ellen said. "My boss is here. I'd better get back to work."

"Nothing pressing," Richard said.

She smiled. "I'm finished. I do need to get back to work. Don't want to take advantage of my boss's good nature."

Good nature, my foot. Perhaps it didn't show, but Richard knew his attitude lately had been anything but good.

"Before you leave, Ellen," Jerry said. "What were you saying about fishing?"

"Dad says if you want to go Saturday, he'd like to fish the Swannanoa River. Jacob can stay with me and play with Missy. So, are we on for Saturday?"

"You bet. Looking forward to it."

Richard ate his lunch, although he had no idea how it tasted. At least he could use the excuse of eating for not talking. Jerry had finished his lunch. As Jerry talked, Richard made a comment or two, but his mind was seeing a replay of the MaryJo incident. This time the picture was Jerry and Ellen. They'd marry. Everyday he would see Ellen. And when they started their family, she'd grow more beautiful every day. They'd have Jacob and Missy and a newborn.

Richard Williams had instigated the whole thing.

They would thank him. . .profusely.

He'd been overjoyed for MaryJo and Ben.

Why wasn't he feeling that about Ellen and Jerry?

"I want to thank you again for getting me and Ellen together," Jerry said. "I would never have made a move toward her." He laughed. "There for awhile I thought you might be interested in her."

"Me?" Richard almost choked on his food. He glanced down. Fish! Good. "Think I swallowed a bone." He took a sip of water, then looked over at his friend. "You know I'm a confirmed bachelor."

"Right." Jerry sat there grinning as if he knew a huge secret. Richard supposed he did. Now that he was seeing Ellen, he'd know much more about her than her boss.

sixteen

Ellen had been thinking about Patsy's situation for several days. On Saturday morning, once her dad and Jerry left to go fishing, she made pancakes for Missy and Jacob. After they discarded their paper plates and she'd wiped the syrup from the table, she asked if they'd like to make cards for a sick woman who had a broken arm and head injury.

The children loved the idea. She'd half-hoped they might say they'd rather watch cartoons, a video, play outside, or even play with Barbies. No such luck. They jumped at the chance. When Ellen said the injured person was Mrs. Hatcher, Missy's little mouth drooped. "Ooooh," she said. "Can we give her flowers?"

"Wonderful idea."

The children made cards from construction paper, markers, and smiley-face stickers that Ellen had saved from an advertisement that had come in the mail. While watching them, Ellen wondered if she should call first.

No, she couldn't chance Patsy saying no.

Heather had said she was more troubled by Patsy's mental outlook than by her physical problems.

"See my card?" Missy smiled, and her blue eyes danced.

Missy had drawn an eye, a heart, and a big U. She put flowers, ranging in color from bright yellow to black, all over the paper.

"Oh, it's beautiful."

Seeing that Jacob was still working on his, Missy said quickly. "I'm not finished. How do you spell "Jesus"?"

Ellen told her.

Missy added, "Jesus, heart, U."

Oh dear, maybe this wasn't such a good idea after all.

129

No, she wouldn't back down. This was a message from Missy. And it was true.

Jacob drew something closely resembling a stick figure with an arm that had squiggly lines going through several places on it. "That's where it's broke." He looked at Ellen for approval.

She gave it, then at his request spelled out "Get well" for him. It looked fine, even though it read "Get mell." She didn't correct him. At a time like this, it really was the thought that counted.

Patsy had a nice brick home in an older residential section of town. As she drove the children to Patsy's address, Ellen warned them that if Patsy wasn't home they would just leave the flowers and cards at the entry. However, she rang the doorbell and after several seconds, Patsy opened the door.

They both looked at each other in silence.

Patsy looked older. Although her hair looked neat, every strand was not in place. She looked pale and thinner than normal. How could she cook, with only a left hand?

A long strip of dark stitches ran across the side of her black, blue, and yellow-green forehead, halfway between her eyebrows and hairline. Dark circles lined her eyes. She wore a loose blouse over slacks. Her right arm, with a cast to the elbow, lay in a sling that draped around her neck.

Would she invite them in?

"Missy and Jacob made cards for you."

Yes, that did it. Patsy would never be rude to a child. "Well, come in," she said softly and smiled at the children. They all stepped into the foyer, and Ellen closed the door behind them. "Now let me see those cards," Patsy said.

Ellen saw Patsy's lips tighten as she looked at Missy's card.

"They designed the cards themselves," Ellen said.

Patsy's quick glance seemed to hold a tinge of amusement. Of course, Patsy would know the children made the cards. But Ellen didn't want Patsy to think she'd prompted the "Jesus loves you" as a reminder of her having been fired.

God, let me not offend her, but let her know I really care.

Patsy praised the children for such thoughtfulness and creativity. "Let's put these in the family room," she said. "Then we'll go into the kitchen and see what kind of surprise we might find for you."

In the family room, she had the children stand their cards up on the desk where several others lay. Two potted plants sat on the desk. "Can we stand these cards up too?" Missy asked.

Patsy said that would be nice.

She led them into the kitchen. "If you'll look under the sink, you'll find some vases."

Ellen found them. She put water in one and arranged the colorful bouquet, then placed it on a small table beneath a window.

"They're beautiful. Thank you so much." Patsy said.

The children were eyeing a plate of brownies. "A neighbor brought those over," Patsy said. "Would you like some?"

The children readily agreed, and Patsy had Ellen tear off a couple of paper towels for them to place their brownies on. Even that small chore would be difficult to do with just one good hand. Ellen felt strange, but good, that Patsy was letting her, even telling her, to get glasses and pour milk for the children. She told them to stay at the table while eating their brownies, then invited Ellen into the sitting room.

Patsy offered Ellen an easy chair, then sat down on the couch, where she leaned back against a pillow. She sighed heavily. "I've never been sick. Now, I feel so. . .helpless."

Helpless? Patsy?

Well, yes, Ellen could see that a vital woman in control of her life and her business would feel terribly helpless under these circumstances.

"I understand a little of how you feel, Patsy. I felt that way when I lost Mom and thought of Missy being without her. That changed my whole life."

"I could empathize to a certain extent, Ellen. I was sorry." She took a deep breath. Ellen had to fight the moisture threatening her eyes when she saw tears in Patsy's eyes. That woman never allowed anyone to see a sign of weakness. She was a very organized, controlled individual with a successful business. And a most difficult business—that of teaching and training little active, energetic children.

"But," Patsy said after a long silent moment. "It's coming closer. My parents, who have always been healthy as horses, are having problems. Mom's memory lapses have become too obvious to be ignored. She's going this week to be tested for dementia. I can't even be there to help right now."

Ellen said softly, "I'm sorry."

She prayed silently as Patsy spoke distantly. "Since Mom's problems began developing, Dad's had difficulty with his breathing."

Knowing Patsy needed to talk to someone, Ellen listened carefully. She almost missed Patsy's near-whisper. "Dad's afraid of hospitals."

Ellen decided to speak. "Well, it's not the most pleasant place."

Patsy looked at her then. "No."

Ellen got a strong feeling Patsy was afraid of hospitals. . .or something. "Can I help in any way? Patsy, I would love to. I had people help me after Mom died. I appreciate that, and it's something I really want to do, if there's any way."

Patsy spread her unbroken hand. "There's nothing anybody can do. I've even been diagnosed with osteoporosis."

Ellen feared saying the wrong thing. "There's medication for that, isn't there?"

Patsy nodded. "Yes, but I've had this for a long time. It was described as mild. Now it's advanced to moderate." She tried to laugh, but the sound came out more like a cry. "I could end up with a hump on my back."

"Maybe not."

Patsy gazed at Ellen for a long moment, then repeated. "Maybe not."

Patsy changed the conversation to Ellen's job. She sounded really interested and pleased for Ellen that things were going well for her and Missy at Ridgeway.

Then Patsy expressed her worries about Little Tykes. "You know Rose, my codirector. She can fill in my job well. My secretary knows how to get things done and consult with me when needed. Even so, I still worry."

Patsy paused, then reached over and touched Ellen's hand. "I want you to know I'm sorry I fired you. If you ever want to come back to Little Tykes, you may."

"Thank you." Ellen felt like Patsy looked as if she'd cry. She thought they were both glad the children came in just then. Ellen said they needed to leave. "But first, we need to make sure the kitchen is clean."

Ellen cleaned up the table and eyed the brownies.

"Why don't you have a brownie, Ellen?" Patsy said.

She did.

When they were ready to leave, the children ran out into the immaculately trimmed lawn and looked at the flower bed. Patsy said, "Ellen, will you. . ." She cleared her throat. "Keep us in your prayers?"

"Yes."

Patsy nodded. "I knew that." She glanced toward the children. "Without asking."

&

Richard marveled at the light in Ellen's eyes the next day at the office when she told him about going to see Mrs. Hatcher and the favorable response she'd received.

"I called her on Sunday and told her I would be bringing dinner tonight. Of course she protested, then said that would be nice."

"She's the one who fired you, right?"

Ellen nodded. "I think she's never really needed anyone before. If she goes to church, I guess they're not bringing in food. Maybe her friends don't realize how incapacitated one can be with a broken arm."

"Hey, you can get supper from the dining hall any time and take it to her."

"Thanks, Richard. Daisy cooks three nights a week, Dad two, and I do weekends." She laughed. "That's why we eat out on Sunday. But it's no trouble cooking a little extra."

"I understand that. But it might be good to let her know other people care. Our singles group could take dinner at least one night a week. I grill a mean steak, remember?"

She smiled. Richard always noticed the way her dimple dented her cheek in such a delightful way.

"Oh, and I wanted to ask you if this would be possible," she added. "Could I take my lunch hour and breaks at one o'clock, to tell the story at Little Tykes, then come back?"

"Yes, Ellen. You may."

"Thank you." She looked relieved. "Patsy needs to know that I forgive her for firing me. She's been open about having made a mistake in doing so. She's asked me to come back, but I don't feel that's right for me. I took that job primarily for Missy's benefit. Things have changed. But if any of my work isn't finished by Fridays, I'll come in on Saturdays."

Richard stood. "Deal." He extended his hand.

She placed her warm soft one in his.

He shouldn't have done that. He wanted to hold her hand longer, to tell her what a wonderful person he thought her to be. He wanted to encourage her. He wanted to—

He let go of her hand and kept the smile pasted on his face, but he looked down at the desk as he sat down in his chair. "Well, I'll let you get back to work. You're doing a great job, Ellen." He tried to sound like a professional boss. Strictly business. He didn't have a friendly personality like Jerry did. Particularly around Ellen, Richard felt he had become a stiff, withdrawn, self-absorbed man.

But not without good reason.

Richard told himself to keep his mind off personal matters and on spiritual ones. "You know, Ellen," he said as she turned toward her office, "this is an example of why we need to let people know where we stand with the Lord. They may reject us, but they know where to turn in time of need. My mom had a neighbor who didn't want to discuss the Lord. But when her sister was diagnosed with brain cancer, she asked Mom to pray for her."

Ellen nodded. "I guess it's true, God works in mysterious ways."

After she went back to her office, Richard considered the mysterious ways God was working in Ellen's life. Ellen was becoming more confident in her work, in herself, with him. When she first came to work, he'd sensed she wanted to be efficient for him. Now it seemed she wanted to be efficient for the job, as it should be. She even had Patsy Hatcher's offer for her job back if she wanted it.

But he missed the way Ellen used to look at him. . .before Jerry. He felt she was separating herself from him. Before, she'd been reluctant to ask to leave a little early. Now she boldly asked so she could help out the woman who'd fired her.

As if feeling his eyes on her, Ellen looked up from her desk, then stood. "Be back in a jif," she said.

After she left her office he stared at her empty chair.

He missed her.

He had gotten an administrative assistant who replaced MaryJo.

Was there one who could replace Ellen if she went back to work at Little Tykes?

He drew in a shaky breath.

He should be happy. He no longer had to worry about any deep feelings for Ellen. He didn't have to worry about having to reveal his past or give up his personal freedom.

Freedom? He laughed inwardly. The brick wall he'd built around himself hadn't crumbled. It was intact. It was his prison. A great loneliness enveloped him.

He'd done himself a great favor.

He'd done his friend Jerry a tremendous favor.

His ploy. . .had worked.

seventeen

Ellen stayed busy. She felt good about Patsy's letting others help her. She liked the work hours too and not having idle time when thoughts of Richard Williams could surface in her mind—just her work. He obviously felt nothing toward her other than as an employer and friend. He'd set her up with Jerry. She should jump at this chance with Jerry. Men like that were rare, she felt sure.

She liked Jerry. He was a wonderful man. A terrific father. A dedicated Christian. But she did not have those special feelings about him. She didn't know how to describe those feelings, but it was something like being in kindergarten and there being one special boy who made her want to please him, to sit near him, and even have him hold her hand.

In college, she'd dated and always asked, "Could I spend my life with him, wake up in the morning lying in the bed beside him?" The answer had always been no. And for the past two years, there hadn't been time or inclination to date. She really hadn't had opportunity to meet any new guys. Suddenly, this summer she'd met two: Richard and Jerry.

Richard wasn't even a consideration if Jerry was right in labeling Richard a confirmed bachelor. Why? Had he just never found the right woman? He had the opportunity to meet many women all the time through conferences and summer programs.

She and Jerry had become close friends. She'd invited him to her home. His son and Missy played well together, a fact that gave the adults a break for a few minutes at a time—at least until someone needed to soothe a hurt, settle a quarrel, put in a video, fix something to eat or drink, or answer two-dozen questions while wiping up a spill.

Jerry and her dad liked to talk. Jerry liked the influence Ellen had on his son. Jerry and Ellen discussed parenting. Did counting to three really work? Spanking? Time out? Being a parent wasn't something that came naturally. He, at least, had to really work at it.

Ellen knew her dad needed to see that she wasn't devoting all her life to Missy. She had activities and people in her life. Her life was full.

She knew Jerry was a wonderful man. There was nothing to detract from him. A woman would be blessed to have a husband like Jerry. *Like* Jerry. Not Jerry himself. He wasn't for her. She wished he were. She wished she wanted to fall into his arms and get that warm, fuzzy feeling she'd heard about. She didn't. To consider that almost seemed to betray their friendship.

⁂

Jon liked the idea of Ellen and Jerry together. However, Jerry seemed to spend more time with him than with Ellen. But the children did have to be supervised, and Ellen enjoyed doing that.

He liked Jerry and would enjoy being a grandparent to Jacob." He mentioned it to Jerry one day while they were fishing.

"That sounds ideal, Jon," Jerry said. "There's just one problem. Ellen and I are not in love with each other."

"Well, what's stopping you from falling in love?"

"I don't know. I think it's called the heart."

Jon looked sideways at Jerry. "What's wrong with you fellas?"

Jerry laughed uncomfortably. "Good question. As far as I can see, there's nothing wrong with Ellen. Any man would be blessed to get her. But Jon, she's not interested in me beyond friendship."

Jon tromped down the stream in his waders and cast the line far out from him. He shook his head. Then he looked over his shoulder and shouted, "It's that boss of hers."

Jerry shrugged. "I can't say. She hasn't told me anything like that."

She hadn't said it in words to Jon either. But it had been in her eyes, in her voice when she'd talked about him before she started up with Jerry. When she spoke of Jerry, her eyes just held warmth. When she spoke of her boss, they held a wistfulness.

Things being so unsettled with Ellen seemed to confirm for Jon that no, it wasn't God's will for Ellen to adopt Missy.

๑

Richard opened his office door after lunch and couldn't believe Ellen and Jerry stood there, embracing. He stared. They broke apart and stared at him, then Ellen sat down as if nothing had happened. Jerry followed when Richard said to him, "Would you come in here, please?"

Jerry walked past him, then Richard shut the door. . .firmly.

Jerry sat in a chair as if nothing was amiss. Trying to control his emotions, Richard paced. "That is not the kind of behavior I tolerate, and you know it."

Jerry sighed. "Can I say something?"

Richard stopped pacing and faced him. "What?"

But he didn't give Jerry time to speak. "That you're sorry? It won't happen again? Forgive you? Forget it?" He shook his head. "Jerry, we don't operate that way here. You know I've sent young people home for any hint of intimacy with each other. Adults have to set the example."

He couldn't believe he heard right when Jerry said, "I'm resigning."

"What?"

"I'm resigning."

Richard shook his head, then put his hand to his forehead. He went over and braced his hands on the window sill and stared out the window. Finally, he went behind the desk and sat. "No, Jerry. I'm wrong here. I made too much of this. Forgive me."

"I'm not angry, Richard. You're right in what you said. And I know what Ellen and I did was perfectly innocent. But I'm resigning."

"Jer—we've been friends for years."

Jerry smiled. "We still are."

"Then why would you let my foolish rantings cause you to leave? Of all people, you know I'm not perfect. And Jerry, my taking out my frustrations on you isn't nearly as bad as some things I've confessed to you. You know how stupid I can be at times."

"Look at me, Richard."

Richard finally fell silent and looked at his friend.

"Do I look mad?"

"Quite the contrary." Richard didn't understand the look on Jerry's face. "Frankly, your expression is annoying."

"Well, I wasn't born to be the most handsome man around, but that's no reason to insult me."

Richard couldn't help but grin and shake his head at his friend of many years. Jerry had often joked about women chasing Richard because they thought him good-looking. But Richard knew his own reserved personality didn't appeal to others the way Jerry's warmth and openness did. "I'm aware you know how to behave in public, Jer. I was off-base. Sometimes things just pile up."

"I know that, Richard. I can't even count the times I've lashed out at you and the world and God after Amy died. You're the one I took my anger out on and sometimes in a way that I made you the object of that anger."

"I understood that, Jerry."

Jerry nodded. "And I understand this."

Richard stared at the knowing eyes of his friend. Knowing, or accusing? Jerry couldn't possibly understand what lay at the bottom of his anger. "Okay, then you forgive me?"

"Sure," Jerry said. "I forgave you before you said it."

"Great. And I forgive you for not resigning. Now, you'd better get back to work before I fire you."

They both laughed.

But Jerry continued to sit. "Richard. My resignation has nothing to do with what went on out there or your reaction.

Jacob is starting public school in the fall. He needs his grand-parents, and they need him. I have decided to go back to my own hometown. I'm ready to live now, Richard. I've lived only for Jacob since Amy died."

They talked for awhile longer, then Jerry rose to leave. Richard again apologized for his outburst. "I don't know what's wrong with me."

Jerry said, "Don't you, Richard? I think it's time we both got over our losses. Ellen taught me that. Her dad taught me that. I think I can move on now. Be ready to relate to a woman in a more personal way if God has that in mind. I never thought I could. Now I do."

He spoke emphatically. "Richard, it's time we both let go of the past."

Jerry didn't close the door when he left Richard's office. Richard watched as Jerry placed his hands on the edge of Ellen's desk and leaned toward her.

Ellen listened attentively to the words that Richard couldn't make out. She smiled and nodded. Jerry smiled and reached over to clasp her hand.

Richard didn't have to hear what was said. He could read the body language. It spoke as loudly as words—perhaps more loudly. He turned toward the window, hoping his face would cool before either Jerry or Ellen might walk into his office.

His eyes lifted toward the opaque white sky. Isn't this where he was supposed to say, "Thank You, Lord"? Isn't this what he wanted when he threw Jerry and Ellen together? Didn't he hope those two deserving people would become a family and then two little children could have two loving parents?

He'd heard the saying, "Be careful what you want. You might get it."

Be happy for them, Richard. This is a good thing. You accomplished something good. They would have found each other without you. But you did play a part. It's your doing. . .

Well, fine. . .

Accept it!

Richard was disgusted with himself. He had no business letting emotion get the better of him this way. He was a matter-of-fact man. Man, yes! Not a kid. He needed to act mature. Be mature.

Determined to obey his mind, which he'd often lost confidence in, he swivelled around again and there stood Jerry, with that unreadable silly expression again. Is that what's called the love expression?

Next, Jerry would probably tell him that he and Ellen were to be married. He'd ask Richard to be the best man.

Best man?

What a joke. *You're the best man, Jer. I'm the worst.*

❧

As usual, July was particularly busy. The center was filled with one big conference after another. Richard had little time for personal pleasure. Jerry was busy getting ready to move as well as taking care of his increased workload that occurred every July as he designed more and bigger brochures for conferences and continued work on the coming year's catalogues.

Richard spent more time in the office with Ellen, as they worked closely together on preparations for the final candlelight service for summer staff.

"All the staff is expected to attend," Richard said. "We like to make this an unforgettable experience." He hoped she might give him a clue if she would be here. Jerry was leaving the day of the service. Neither of them had been as open with each other since Jerry and Ellen had become close.

Now, Ellen just nodded that she understood.

"Also," Richard said. "You can start organizing the list for making appointments at colleges for my recruitment of summer staff. That will begin in the fall after school starts." He watched her making notes. "Are you planning to return to school this fall?"

She glanced up at him and back at her notepad. "I'm not sure yet."

"You'll let me know?"

He wanted to know if she and Jerry were serious. Or if she was going leave him and return to school. But she gave no clue.

"Sure I'll let you know," she said. The phone rang, and she turned to answer it. Richard returned to his office.

He regretted that Ellen had moved away from him emotionally. But he had no one to blame but himself. He'd pushed her away. He should have been honest with her from the beginning. But then, that might require being honest with himself.

Now, he must get back to the way things were before Ellen came into his life.

Back to business. . .as usual.

eighteen

Ellen still loved her job but wondered about the wisdom of working so closely with Richard. Her feelings for him were growing stronger, rather than weaker. She honestly didn't know what to do about work or school. She kept praying for a sign.

In the meantime, she counted her blessings, knowing they were numerous, and she had little choice but to stay busy. She rarely saw Heather, who was over her head in finishing her thesis and studying for the pass-fail comps she'd have to take in a few months.

One Friday evening in mid-July, Ellen took supper to Patsy and sat across the table from her, drinking a cup of coffee.

"You're looking good, Patsy," Ellen could honestly say. The bruises had vanished, the stitches had been removed, and the red streak was fading. She'd gained some weight back.

"Thank you," she said, "but Ellen, what's bothering you? You're not your old cheerful self."

Ellen didn't want to share her feelings about Richard with anyone. She needed to stay focused on the more pressing issue. She knew Patsy cared about Missy.

"Dad has invited Leanne, Missy's birth mother, to come and visit. That bothers me. What if Leanne wants Missy now?"

Patsy listened intently to all Ellen said about the matter. "Ellen, I can't say what is best. But the Lord knows. I could tell you were devastated when I fired you. But God worked that for good, didn't He?"

Ellen nodded. Even if there could never be a relationship with Richard beyond friendship, she wasn't sorry for having known him. He was a wonderful man, who considered his job a service for the Lord. But what did Patsy know about the workings of the Lord?

"You're surprised, Ellen," Patsy said, as if she'd read Ellen's mind. "Let me explain. When I was principal of the primary school, I had to be so careful to avoid offending someone of another faith. But things have gotten so out-of-hand, Ellen. Everyone can be open about their faith except Christians."

Ellen knew how that felt. It had happened to her at Little Tykes.

"Yes, I do believe in God," Patsy continued. "One would have to be an idiot to think this world came from a big bang, and a human being was once a fish in the ocean. I mean, where'd the stuff come from to bang and where'd that single cell come from? It just happened?" she scoffed.

Ellen smiled.

Patsy's voice lowered, as if trying to keep from startling Ellen further. "I even believe Jesus is the Son of God. I was jealous of your openness about your personal relationship with Him. I'd become conditioned to saying that's private. What I really was saying is that my faith wasn't top priority."

Ellen saw a tear roll from the corner of Patsy's eye and got up to get a tissue. This was so unlike the woman. She never cried to anyone.

"I couldn't have children. I wanted that more than anything. My husband wanted a family. I was jealous. You lost your mother, but you had a beautiful child. I love children."

"You're good with children, Patsy. They love you."

Patsy nodded. "I've decided to quit blaming God because I was barren." She took in a deep breath, then exhaled. "Firing you was a mean thing."

"Patsy, I forgive you. Maybe you need to rest. We can talk about this—"

Patsy was shaking her head. "Please, I need to say this."

"Okay."

"Firing you turned out to be one of the best things that could have happened to me. My conscience wouldn't let me be. Or maybe more accurately, God wouldn't let me be."

Ellen reached over and squeezed her hand. "Then I think

I served my purpose—or God's—in working for you for two years."

Patsy smiled. "I've decided I should let the world and the children know that I am a Christian. I know that some of them don't go to church, because they talk about where they went over the weekend. I need to be open about my beliefs. Not force it on any child, but let it be what I believe and leave it up to the parents what to do with that information. Forgive me, but at the time, I said to myself, 'What does that young, uneducated whippersnapper Ellen know about life and raising children?' "

"I do forgive you. And I don't know a lot about raising children. I have to learn as I go."

"We all do," Patsy admitted. "I wanted to hurt you by saying you're not a mother. But you are. You have a mother's heart, a mother's instinct toward Missy."

Ellen replied, "Like you've had with hundreds of children, thousands really."

"It's what I like to believe," Patsy said. "And don't you forget, you have a job at Little Tykes, if you ever want it."

❧

Ellen could go back to Little Tykes. She'd liked it there.

She liked the job at Ridgeway, even if she could never be more than friends with Richard. It was a worthwhile job working with an organization whose purpose was to attract people to the Lord Jesus Christ and strengthen their faith.

She could easily have fallen in love with Richard. Now that she'd been forced to take a few steps backward and analyze her feelings, her deeper desires surfaced. If Richard wasn't the man God had chosen for her, or she was not the woman He'd chosen for Richard, then God had someone else in mind for her—she hoped. If not, she could devote her life to making a difference in the lives of others, as Richard had apparently done.

Just raising Missy in the admonition of the Lord had been a full-time, most rewarding project. She smiled at the thought.

She was still smiling when she opened the kitchen door,

saw the stack of mail on the table, and opened the letter from New York addressed to Ellen and Jon Jonsen.

Dear Uncle Jon and Ellen,

Thanks loads for inviting me to visit.

I can fly down as soon as there's a break in my soap story. You know, they jump from one thing to another, and others on the soap have the leading story at times. Right now, it's mine. So, I'll let you know.

Love,
Leanne

P.S. I have a man in my life finally. Hector Myers, known as Rock Samson on Love's Sweet Promise. *He's the one with the muscles.*

Ellen had ceased to smile. She remembered her dad being concerned about what kind of man would raise Missy. What more could one want than a rock with muscles! She told herself not to be sarcastic. More seriously, she wondered what all her dad had said to Leanne.

She asked him after Missy went to bed.

"Ellen, I've agonized over this. I've been reluctant to consider changing our situation. Missy is my daughter. I've asked Daisy if she would help me raise her. She doesn't feel up to taking her on as a full-time responsibility any more than I do. It's not that I don't want to. I'm just not the best person for her."

Ellen felt the frustration welling up in her again. "And you don't think I am."

"Oh, Ellen. I know you are. That's not the problem. And Jerry has helped me see that a single parent can do a great job with a child. You've proved it for the most part during the past two years. But I am not convinced it's best for you."

"It's what I want, Dad."

He sighed. "I know. But this decision is mine to make, not yours. I have to live with giving my little girl to someone else.

I want to do the right thing for everyone, and what that right thing is simply isn't clear to me yet."

Ellen began to understand that her dad's struggles were not against her or her ability to be a mom. "Dad, I'm sorry I haven't been more sympathetic."

But she couldn't bear to think of Missy leaving them. "Dad, you're great with Missy. Can we just leave everything like it is? If I ever do marry, I'd still be part of Missy's life. Let's just not make any hasty decisions."

He was nodding, but the look on his face didn't reflect agreement. "I've struggled with this for a long time, Ellen. In all good conscience, I have to give Leanne the opportunity to settle this once and for all. I know it's settled legally, but if that girl changes her mind and wants Missy, then it can cause all kinds of trouble for us. It's different since your mom died. I've seen situations on TV and read in the news about parents showing up later in a child's life and gaining custody. I don't want to chance that."

"I understand that, Dad. But you're forcing the issue. Leanne has seen pictures of Missy, and she's never indicated she wants her."

"She's nineteen now, Ellen. And her letter made it sound like she is thinking of serious relationships. She's not a fourteen-year-old girl anymore." His eyes became teary. "This breaks my heart, Ellen."

Tears stung Ellen's eyes as well. She hadn't seen her dad cry since her mom died. She began to realize how he agonized over the situation. She began to see the situation from his point of view. Her dad didn't think her a terrible mom. He just wanted to do the right thing for both his daughters.

He opened his arms to Ellen, and she fell into them. They hugged each other more tightly than they had in a long time.

❧

Richard helped with the planning for the going-away luncheon the department heads would have for Jerry on his last day at Ridgeway, but he still wanted to do something special with Jerry apart from that. Before he decided what to do, Jerry came up to him after church.

"Let's have lunch together, Richard. Jacob's going home with his friend Chris for the afternoon."

Richard wanted to spend time with his friend, but he hoped he wouldn't end up hearing all about the growing relationship between Jerry and Ellen. They were two of the most wonderful people he knew, and already he felt the loss of them both.

Since the two men ate daily at the Ridgeway cafeteria, they opted for the Fish Camp, where they could be waited on. They sat in a booth by a window with a view of a deep green boxwood hedge bordering the parking lot and beyond that the main road with the mountains in the background.

Richard knew Jerry liked the mountains. "Think you can adjust to being away from here?"

Jerry scoffed. "You're my best friend. I plan to come back and visit often."

Richard felt uneasy, thinking of Jerry and Ellen in his home as a married couple. "You're always welcome. But it would be a little strange to have you at my home with a wife."

Jerry stared at him the entire time the waitress set their plates in front of them. As soon as she moved away, Jerry said, "A wife? Does that mean you have someone else in mind to set me up with?"

Richard stared at him. "Uh. . .let's pray." He quickly added, "You pray."

Jerry asked God's blessing on the food, then looked across at Richard with a dumbfounded expression. "I should have prayed for your sanity, Richard."

"What do you mean?" Richard unwrapped his silverware from the cloth napkin.

"I mean, there's nothing beyond friendship between me and Ellen. I knew you were just trying to back away, like you've always done when it seems you or a woman might start getting serious."

Richard poised his fork over the fish. "You know me too well."

"Fortunately." Jerry picked up a fried shrimp, dipped it in sauce, and took a bite. After a moment, he spoke. "If either Ellen or I didn't care about you, then that situation might have been ideal. We like each other, Richard. But I'm your friend. You and Ellen will have to deal with what you are to each other."

Richard took a bite of his fried oysters. "Good," he said, while chewing, wondering if Jerry would believe his pleasure was because of the food.

He didn't. "Richard, it's time you dealt with your problem and let it go. Ellen and her dad are the kind of people who can understand what you've been through."

"I've dealt with it." Richard poked his oysters with his fork. "I think Ellen likes me and respects me. But why should I tell her something that's going to make her lose respect for me? I mean, look at her. She's gorgeous, makes all the right decisions. How could she accept my past?"

"Oh, Richard. You just don't know. She has her faults."

Richard straightened. "What faults?"

Jerry put his fork down and laid his hand on the table near his plate. He began to tap on the table with his index finger. "She does that when she's thinking or agitated."

Richard stared at him. "You're kidding."

"Nope." Jerry picked up his fork and started eating again.

"Jerry. That's nothing. I'm a drummer, remember."

Jerry looked across at him quickly and with food in his mouth said, "Well. That sounds like a match made in heaven to me."

Richard finished his meal, thinking it was the best he'd eaten in a long time.

❧

On Monday, Ellen felt the pressure of constant activities at work. All departments cooperated in dealing with conferences, big and small, which created a constant flow of people coming and going. Richard had said July would be the most hectic month, and she'd discovered that was an understatement. Besides daily business, there was the planning for the final candlelight service for the summer staff around the lake.

She and Richard hardly had time to acknowledge each other's presence, until he said, "It mustn't rain on closing night. You put in an order for a clear sky."

She laughed. That felt good. There hadn't been either time or inclination for much laughter. Also she was working on setting up his recruitment appointments.

After lunch, she was needed for a couple of hours to help with registering conferees.

"Your dad called," Richard said when she got back to the office.

She returned the call and slumped into her desk chair when her father asked if she could pick up Leanne from the airport. Her flight would arrive at 4:14. Daisy was cooking dinner for them all. He'd already gotten Missy from preschool. "Do you mind?" he asked.

"Hold on," she said. "Let me ask."

"I know it's our busiest time," she said as she walked into Richard's office. She told him why she needed to leave within thirty minutes.

"You may leave now, if that helps," he said. "Come back in after you hang up with your dad."

Minutes later, she went back into his office and stood beside his desk, looking out the window.

"We haven't talked for awhile, Ellen, about the situation with your dad and Missy. I just wanted you to know I care, and I've been praying about it."

"Thanks." She tried to force down the flood of emotion she feared might erupt. "I appreciate that. I'm beginning to understand my dad, although I still think he's wrong. What do you think? Should he even consider bringing Leanne into this?"

Richard rose from his chair and went over and closed the door. He stared at the floor as he paced a few steps. "Ellen, it seems to me that a child who has had one loving home for over four years, shouldn't be uprooted. At the same time, I can sympathize with parents who might want their child, even if they haven't seen the child in over four years. At the same time, I know what this is doing to you. I know."

The way he said it made her believe he really understood. "Richard, do you know firsthand about these types of situations?"

Suddenly, she felt like a curtain closed between them. He took a step, as if to walk away from her. She saw the rise of his shoulders. Then he turned toward her again. His dark eyes seemed filled with pain. After releasing a deep breath he said, "Ellen, I can empathize to a certain extent. There is something I would like to tell you. It's a situation that comes between us, totally because of me. Right now, I would like to tell you. Maybe that's because you have to leave and there isn't time."

"I wish you could confide in me," she said sincerely.

He nodded. "I would like to. In another sense, it's something I don't like facing over and over. It's done. It's unchangeable, but it haunts me." He shrugged. "But you don't need the burden of my confession. You have your own problems."

"Oh, Richard. Maybe I can't solve your problems. But it's meant so much to me when you've listened about how I hurt when I think of Missy being taken from me. I can't handle my concerns by myself. It helps just to talk about it and get another's opinion."

"I know," he said. "I've talked with Jerry. That was hard, but in a way it was a release. If ever there's one in whom I could confide, Ellen, it would be you. I have been praying about this and will continue to until I feel peace about disclosing something this personal that happened in my past."

"The past is forgiven," she said. "It's over."

"Yes," he said. "But think of it this way. If your cousin thinks she made a mistake for giving up her child, she could be forgiven. But there are still issues to be dealt with and decisions to be made. A beautiful child's future must be decided. I wish I had the answer. But I'm sorry. I can't be objective about this situation. If Missy were yours, and you were the one who had given her up, do you suppose you would not have thought of her, wanted her, even if you had done the right thing at age fourteen?"

Ellen hadn't wanted to look at it that way. "Oh, Richard. You're right. I wish you weren't. I can see that my desires may be selfish."

He shook his head. "No. I think your desires are based on having become Missy's mom in every way except having given birth to her."

"But I need to think of other people too. Leanne's only nineteen. I wasn't very mature at nineteen. But I'm sure her situation at fourteen matured her in many ways. Just as my mom's death and my home situation matured me."

Richard nodded. "I understand. These jolts in life have a way of making us face ourselves in a different, more mature way and realize how much we need God to be in our lives, not just on the periphery."

Ellen knew Richard had a great strength within him. She was so quick to tell whomever would listen about her problems. She wished Richard would confide in her. At the same time, she admired his maturity in trying to be sure that he should share his burden.

She didn't think about what happened next. She just went over to Richard, and when she came close, he opened his arms to her, like her dad had done. The embrace felt like friends consoling friends.

After a long moment, he released her. His lips brushed hers for the briefest moment, then he held her at arm's length. "Ellen," he said. "As much as I would like it to be different, I know what is between us must come to a stop unless I can be honest with you about myself. Now you'd better leave, or you'll be late."

She nodded.

Richard did care for her. But what terrible thing had he done that so disturbed him?

&

On the way to the airport, Ellen gave herself a good lecture.

She began to see that her motives in wanting Missy to be hers had been based on what she believed was right and good. But she hadn't considered the distress all this had caused her dad.

Ellen had agonized over possibly losing Missy. She hadn't considered that Leanne might have agonized over having given up Missy. And she had been more concerned about her own situation than about picking up on the distress in Richard's life.

"I'm trying, God. I'm giving it to You," she said aloud while speeding along the interstate. At least she said the words, even if her heart still held on. She wanted Missy. She believed Missy needed her more than anyone. Well, no, she needed her Pa-Pa too. Ellen began to realize her dad was going through the same kind of agony as she.

She recognized beautiful Leanne immediately, although she hadn't seen her in more than four years. She'd seen the younger girl in photos and a couple of times on the TV soap opera.

They hugged.

Ellen began to realize that Leanne was more nervous than she.

"You think I'm awful, don't you?" Leanne said as soon as they were settled in the car.

That surprised Ellen. "Why would I think that?"

She could barely hear Leanne, who spoke softly when she said, "Because I gave up my own baby."

"No," was all Ellen could say for a moment. She focused on the road in front of the airport and on making her turns before pulling out onto the main road. Again, it struck her how she had not considered others' feelings the way she should. Her mom and dad had sent pictures of Missy to Leanne. Ellen had never written a letter to Leanne or acknowledged that Leanne's heart might be broken by her sacrifice.

Ellen began to talk honestly and listen attentively to this young girl who had lost what had become most precious to Ellen. Finally, Leanne said she always thought she'd done the right thing.

"But I've lived a life of pretense," she said. "In high school,

I went to ball games, acted in all the plays, and pretended I was just another teenager." She shook her head.

Ellen glanced over and saw the tears on Leanne's cheek.

"I know," Leanne said after taking a tissue and dabbing at her eyes, "that Uncle Jon wants me to take Missy now."

"Oh no," Ellen said quickly. Then she stopped to think how to say this without imposing her own desires. "He just wants you to have the opportunity. He thinks you should see her and settle this once and for all."

"We did that when Missy was born," Leanne said.

"I know, Leanne. But our situation changed. Dad thinks yours may have also. But I want you to know that I am selfish enough to want Missy as my own. I feel like she's my own."

"I do too," Leanne said. "Your dad has written about how you took over after Aunt Mary died. You're in the same position I was in when I gave her up."

"Not really." Ellen paused as she turned onto the interstate. "You were younger. Didn't want a lasting relationship with Missy's dad. You said you weren't ready. Leanne, I am ready. Missy was my little sister for two years. For the past two years, she has been my daughter."

"Do you think maybe you're trying to fill the void of losing your mom?"

"No." Ellen could answer that without hesitation. "Nothing can fill the void left by my mom's death. And to be honest, I don't need Missy in my life to be fulfilled."

Ellen had to stop and let her throat clear before she could go on. The emotion was just too great. She tried again. Her chest hurt. "If you take her, I would be devastated. In my heart, she is my child. But I also love her enough to accept giving her to you, if that's what you and Dad decide is best."

Leanne sat silent for a long moment. Then she took a deep breath and spoke again. "I don't know how I will feel when I see Missy for the first time."

❧

When they arrived home, Leanne embraced her uncle Jon.

Ellen then introduced her to Daisy and Missy.

"Missy, this is my cousin, Leanne."

"Hey, My-cuz-in."

They all laughed. Ellen explained that "My-cuz-in" wasn't Leanne's name. She was a relative, like an aunt or uncle.

Missy's eyes brightened. "Oh, yes. I have two cousins. They're in. . . Where are they, Mommy?"

Ellen dared not look at Leanne to see her reaction to Missy calling her Mommy. "Bret and Rita are in Arkansas."

"Yeah. Arkansas."

Leanne smiled. "You're adorable."

Missy took on her sassy attitude. "I'm Missy."

"An adorable Missy."

"And you're My-cuz-in." She giggled.

They sat down to supper, and Missy did what she loved doing when allowed—talk constantly. She told about her school, fishing, friends, and church. Ellen watched Leanne for reactions. She could tell Leanne loved Missy from the moment she saw her, and her wonder at the little girl seemed to grow.

Ellen also noticed that Leanne ate very little of her supper. Was it because of inner turmoil or was she simply watching her calories?

After supper, Leanne leaned back in her chair. "My flight goes out tonight at nine-thirty. Uncle Jon, could I talk with you?"

"Let's walk," he said.

Ellen and Daisy cleaned up the kitchen, while Missy dressed her Barbies for Leanne to see when she returned from her walk.

After they came back and Missy showed her Barbies, Dad said, "Missy, let's let Ellen and Leanne talk awhile. You, me, and Daisy can get some lemonade and go outside to the swing set. What do you say?"

"Oh, neat!"

"By that response," Ellen said, "you'd think this was her first time on the swing set instead of it being something she plays with several times a day."

Ellen dreaded the wistful look in Leanne's eyes as her gaze followed the gray-haired man and little tow-headed girl as they walked out into the backyard.

"You guys have done a great job with her," Leanne said. She sighed. "I talked to Hector about it. His career is just taking off like mine. He doesn't think marriage is best at this time, much less taking on the responsibility of a child. I don't even have mom to help me. She's tied up with her work and her own life. Like you said, Uncle Jon is trying to do the right thing. I think he has all along, Ellen, and so have you."

Ellen held her breath. Was Leanne saying what Ellen hoped she was saying?

"I'm so glad you want her, Ellen. You or your dad, either one. When he called me, I thought he wanted me to take her. But in my line of work, raising a child would be difficult. Especially a child who doesn't know me."

"Do you think," Leanne said, tears filling her eyes, "someday you could let her know about me? That I. . .loved her?"

Ellen breathed a sigh of relief and a thankful prayer. "Yes, we can do that."

nineteen

If everyone lit just one little candle, what a bright world this would be.

The line of that song ran through Ellen's mind as she stood in the last row of hundreds of people, each holding a candle, gathered around the lake at the boys' camp. This service marked the end of the summer season.

It might mark the end of her summer season too. So much had happened—losing and regaining a relationship with Patsy, fearing losing Missy but coming to an understanding with her dad, not really losing Richard because he'd never been hers. The past week had been too busy for confidences, other than her briefly telling him that she and her dad were seriously talking now about Missy's future without Leanne being an issue. Richard had been pleased, but he hadn't confided in her about himself.

The song leader led the group in the season's theme song, "Jesus is the Light of the World."

I can do all things with Christ's help. The verse ran through Ellen's mind. She'd lived without her mom. Her dad had said he wouldn't try to force Ellen into a relationship or a career but would just let her make her own decisions.

What did God have for her? The words of the song rang through the night. She couldn't help the emotion that welled up in her. She felt God's peace, but at the same time, her heart was filled with thoughts of her mom; Leanne, who didn't have her child with her; and Richard with whatever secret he harbored. She turned and stepped away from the crowd gathered around the lake.

She was startled to see Richard. Apparently, he'd been standing back from the crowd, behind her. She looked up at

157

him, knowing her eyes were moist. She couldn't speak.

He reached out his hand. "Could I talk with you, Ellen?"

Unable to find words, she nodded and put her hand in his.

They walked together along the shadowed path, where moonlight filtered down through the overhanging tree limbs.

❧

Richard knew he could only tell Ellen in the dark. He wished he could be telling her he loved her and wanted to spend the rest of his life with her and Missy. But a night that might have been romantic was instead a night to face the consequences of his past. This would put an end to his own longing that could never be fulfilled.

Jerry had always said Richard got cold feet when anything more serious than friendship threatened to develop between him and a woman. Now his feet felt like ice!

But as they walked along the path toward the picnic area, Richard knew if he didn't face this now, he never would. The sound of singing faded in the background, replaced by the flow of babbling water in the creek.

Now that he'd decided to talk, he knew no other way than to just say it. "Ellen, my withdrawal from close personal relations began with four words spoken by my girlfriend when we were in college. She said, 'I've had an abortion.'" He admitted what hurt so much. "Because of my callousness, she did that. She wanted me to love her. And I made it clear I didn't want a baby. Before I even had a chance for the news of her pregnancy to sink in, she had the abortion. But her choice was my fault. I had told her that I loved her, but my reaction to her pregnancy showed anything but love. I didn't tell her to have an abortion. But I caused her to make that choice by my attitude."

❧

Ellen felt Richard's sorrow as he walked over and slumped down on the seat of a picnic table. She sat beside him. "Did you ask God to forgive you?"

"Over and over," he said.

"And how many times does it take before He forgives you?"

A scoffing, laughing sound emerged from his throat. "Well. Come on, Ellen."

"I mean it, Richard. How much begging do you have to do before God forgives you?"

"You know the answer to that."

She spoke softly. "I would like to hear you say it."

He sighed heavily. "Of course He has."

Richard's face was in shadows. She could hear the anguish in his voice. "Because of me, my own baby. . .was murdered."

Ellen didn't know how she could reply to that. He believed abortion was murder. His baby had been aborted. "But you didn't do it. And God will forgive your girlfriend if she asks."

"I believe that," he said. "But she did it because of my reluctance to admit or take responsibility. I could have said I'd marry her. Or that I would take care of the baby. My parents would have done that. Just like your parents wanted to take Missy. Mine would have helped in any way. But I was irresponsible."

He took a deep breath, and his next words sounded shaky. "I'm responsible for the murder of my own flesh and blood."

Silence. Crickets. Frogs. The rushing water a background for what? To Richard, was it all a condemnation?

Jesus came to give living water—forgiveness.

"Richard, I've sinned too. I've done the usual things teens get into, and in college I went further than high school days in many areas. Even today, I speed on the interstate. I lose my temper. I have thoughts I shouldn't have and sometimes entertain them instead of getting rid of them. Right after Patsy fired me, I hated her for what she was doing to me and Missy, how she had disrupted the routine we'd seemed to be settling into after Mom died."

He scoffed. "Ellen. That's nothing compared with what I've done. What I have to live with."

"Isn't it?" She felt herself becoming angry. "Did Jesus die only for the people who speed or steal a twenty-dollar bill or curse?"

"Come on."

"No, Richard. He died for every sin, or none at all. I can't say a person gets forgiven for speeding, but not for. . ." She hated the word but knew he had said it. Taking a deep breath, she continued. "Not for murder. Do you believe people in prison can be forgiven for murder?"

"Yes," Richard answered. "If they're truly repentant and proclaim the Lord Jesus as their Savior and change their ways. Ellen, I've known these things all my life. I could answer any of the basic Bible questions that you could ask me."

"Oh, it's just you who can't be forgiven then?"

"Okay, Ellen. You want me to say it. Yes, God forgave me. But I can't forgive myself. I try. No, I don't go around thinking about it. But it's like my heartbeat. It's a part of me."

"And you're trying to punish yourself by never getting married. Never having a child."

"I want those things, Ellen. I just can't see anyone respecting me after knowing this about me. I've never told anyone except Jerry."

"Why are you telling me?"

"Because I care for you and every day that caring grows deeper. I want to be near you, around you. And I have to do something to make you go away from me. I wouldn't have to tell you if you married Jerry, but you didn't. I wouldn't have to tell you if MaryJo returned, but she didn't. And it's ridiculous to fire you and get someone else now that you know the job. I feel I owe you an explanation for my actions, although I have to face the fact that you can never respect me again, that there's no chance for the two of us together."

No chance? Her heart beat fast at the prospect of every chance. But at the moment, this conversation was not about her. Richard was confiding in her, like a friend would do. She must keep her focus on that.

"Richard, what would you say to one of your college staff in this situation?"

"I would tell them to accept God's forgiveness, forgive themselves, and go on with life. I know those things. I don't listen to my own counsel." He turned his hand over and held hers. "Now that I've told you, I realize even more that the problem lies within myself. I remember the last time I saw Colleen, we were in a screaming match. She was telling me what she thought of me, which wasn't much, and I was blaming her and killing her heart with my words."

"Richard, have you forgiven Colleen for killing your baby?"

He shook his head. "I've tried."

Ellen laid her hand on his shoulder. "I hope you find it in your heart to forgive her."

Richard nodded. "I have to find a way to let go of this, so I can go on with my life."

"Richard," she said softly. "I respect you for admitting this. I can see how hard that is for you. I just want you to know that I think you're a wonderful man."

❧

Richard awoke in the middle of the night with Colleen on his mind. He also thought of Mark Freedlan. Mark had been a friend of his at the university. Now he was a college professor there. They hadn't kept in touch, but Richard received a form letter from the university each year about alumni gatherings which Richard had ignored.

Early in the morning, although having no idea what time Mark might leave home for the university or how far from it he lived, Richard called the university. He drummed his fingers on the countertop while listening to numerous computerized responses until he realized that this was exactly what callers got when they called Ridgeway, unless they knew the number of a person in a particular department.

Finally, he managed to reach a person who connected him to Dr. Freedlan's voice phone. Richard left his name and number.

That evening, Mark called, excited to hear from him.

"We'll have to get together one of these days and talk over old times," Mark said. Richard heard children and activity in the background. Mark said he had married and they had two young children.

They got to talking about some of their old friends and acquaintances. Mark mentioned a girl he'd dated who married a guy they both knew.

"Any idea whatever happened to Colleen?" Richard asked.

"Colleen?" Mark hesitated for a moment. "Oh, yeah. You dated her for awhile, didn't you? She's a doctor at Mission Hospital, here in this city. Still single, last I knew. She's come to a few of our alumni meetings. Something I can't say for everybody I know."

Richard laughed with him and talked awhile longer. They both promised to drop in on each other if they were in their respective areas.

Richard knew he had enough information.

The following morning, he asked and received permission from the director to take a couple day's leave to handle a personal matter. It would be a four-hour drive. He told Ellen where he was going.

She'd nodded, but her expression seemed to ask what he felt inside—where would this lead?

৯

While Richard was away from the office, Ellen continued preparations for the fall term. But as she worked, she kept wondering if Richard had found his college sweetheart. Would she be married? Would she still be in love with Richard? And he with her? Would they renew their relationship?

If that's what was needed for Richard to forgive himself and to allow a woman in his life to bring fulfillment and children, then she wanted that for him. Yes, even as it broke her heart to think of it, she loved him enough to want what was best.

Ellen shook her head. The truth was she wanted her own will to be done. Richard Williams was in her heart and mind. She wanted him to love her and for them to build a life together.

Even as she wanted that, she prayed as she knew she must. *Dear God, Thy will be done.*

twenty

Ellen was all nerves on Saturday night while waiting for Richard to pick her up. He'd called the night before to let her know he was back, then had asked if she would have dinner with him at the Eclectic. He drove to her house, came inside, and met her dad.

Ellen hoped her dad wouldn't say anything too personal to Richard. He'd already said to her, "He's the one you've been interested in all along. Right?"

"He's my boss and my friend," she'd said.

Her dad had nodded. "And one of those confirmed bachelor guys." He'd laughed then.

When he met Richard, however, he said nothing to embarrass her.

Ellen and Richard made small talk on the way to the restaurant. They talked about the work at Ridgeway while he was gone, how things were going for her with her dad, and even the weather. Ellen longed to question him about Colleen but decided to be patient.

After they were seated, Ellen thought how different this was from when she'd sat in this same restaurant with Jerry. Soft candlelight and music set the stage for her and the man she loved. Richard looked more peaceful than ever before. Was it because of Colleen? Had they renewed their relationship?

After their order came, Richard began to talk about the trip. "I talked with Colleen," he said. "She forgave me years ago. She said that tragic event caused her to give her life to the Lord and seek a profession in pediatrics, where she can help little children through their illnesses. She teaches a class of young girls in Sunday school."

Seeing his enthusiasm, she had to ask, "Are you still in love with her?"

"No," he said, putting down his fork. "Colleen is a wonderful Christian woman, but she's not the woman I love." He paused, reached across the table, and captured her hand with both of his.

"There's only one woman in the world I love and want to spend the rest of my life with," he said softly.

Ellen looked down at her plate, not able to bear the tenderness in his gaze as he studied her face.

"Please look at me," he whispered.

Feeling unexpectedly shy, she looked up at him.

"Ellen Jonsen," he said quietly, "I'm in love with you."

"Oh, Richard. I love you too."

Tenderly, he caressed her hand. "I don't know if I can finish this dinner. I'm eager to hold a woman in my arms without that terrible anguish of holding back."

She gave him a warning look but smiled. "Well, I don't know about that."

He laughed and shook his head. "I mean holding back my awful secret. I know for now I must settle for a hug and kiss. . . until marriage."

"Marriage?" She could hardly believe that after so many months of being so reserved, he was ready to make such a commitment.

"Ellen, when I think of us together, and I do often, I want to spend the rest of my life with you."

Ellen thought her heart would burst with joy as she and Richard spent the remainder of the meal revealing how they had come to recognize their love for each other. But before the evening ended with a prolonged kiss at Ellen's doorstep, the couple had also agreed on the importance of Richard spending more time with both Ellen's dad and with Missy.

"Your dad can't consider me as a prospective father for Missy until he knows me better," Richard stated. "And even if he agrees to let us adopt that little girl, we can't do something that will create so many changes in her life until I spend more time with her and she can get used to the idea."

≈

Over the next few weeks, Richard visited Ellen's family many times. Miss Daisy often joined them. After several visits, Richard took Ellen's father aside and told him of his past, then asked if he could approve of him as a son-in-law and a prospective dad for Missy.

"Well, I think this is something Ellen and Daisy should hear," Jon said.

Jon told Missy to play with her Barbies for awhile. The adults gathered around the kitchen table.

Richard had no idea what might ensue. He watched Jon look around at each one, then focus on Richard. "I have no problem with you as a son-in-law. Or with Ellen as Missy's mom."

Richard glanced at Ellen and saw the joy in her eyes. Then Jon focused on Richard again. "However, Missy will have to make a transition from here to your house. That may need to be done slowly. Of course, I don't have any reason to change her room. It's not likely Daisy will have any more children."

"Jon!"

He ignored Daisy's outburst and continued. "Missy can live at both places." He addressed Richard. "You'll need a transition period too. Get used to having a little girl around." He looked over the top of his eyeglasses and spoke ominously. "The biggest transition is having a big girl around."

Richard grinned. "Looking forward to it."

"Yes, I know the feeling. It's happened twice in my life."

"Twice?" Ellen questioned. She'd never heard that.

"Yep. With your mother. Now Daisy."

"Dad! You and Daisy. . . ?"

"If I can talk her into it, we'll get us a motor home and tour the U-S of A."

Daisy tugged on his shirt sleeve. "Um, Jon. Would you let me drive some of the time? I just don't like the way you tailgate."

"Sure." He gave her a sidelong look. "Might as well be in the driver's seat as to sit over there beside me telling me how to do it." He grinned and winked at Ellen and Richard.

Daisy sighed heavily. "It's about time I got through to him. He thinks he's going to talk me into it. Men! He has no idea I've been here for two years not because I like to clean his house and cook. He'll learn. I like to watch TV and work jig-saw puzzles as much as he does."

"I make up my own mind about things, Woman," Jon said.

Daisy looked toward the ceiling, then sat there grinning.

"There is one more thing," Richard said. "How Missy feels will play a big part in this."

Ellen stood. "I'll get her."

After Missy came in, holding her Barbie, Richard asked, "How would you feel about my being your daddy?"

"I have a Pa-Pa." she said. "I want to stay with Mommy and Pa-Pa."

Richard felt his heart stop. This wasn't going to work after all.

"Well, I was thinking of marrying your mommy. She'd still be your mommy. Your Pa-Pa would still be your Pa-Pa, but you would live with your mommy and me."

Missy glanced around at each of them. Then she looked up at Richard with her big blue eyes shining like he'd given her the world.

She looked at Ellen. "She would still be my mommy?" She pointed to Jon. "You would be my Pa-Pa? She looked at Richard. "And you would be my daddy?"

He nodded. "That's right."

Her cheeks dimpled, and she said, "Okay. Now can I go play?"

epilogue

The wedding ceremony had been beautiful, and at last the pastor declared, "I now pronounce you husband and wife. You may kiss the bride."

Ellen faced Richard, looking up at him with her heartfelt love shining in her eyes. As much as he wanted to whisk her away and kiss her in private, he had something else he must do first. "Not just yet," he whispered to Ellen.

He motioned Missy to come over from the spot where she stood as a flower girl, then he got on his knees in front of her. "I promise, Missy, to be your dad. I will be to you the best dad I know how."

Richard reached for her left hand and held it in his left one. Then he reached into the pocket of his tux and drew out a small gold band. "With this ring, I promise to love and cherish you as long as we both shall live."

He slipped the ring on the finger next to her little pinkie.

Her face looked as if the sun had risen inside her. She threw her arms around his neck and hugged him. Then she kissed his cheek. "I love you, Daddy."

"And I love you, Missy."

"Oh," she said, "now can I go to your moon with you?"

⁂

Richard and Ellen had decided on a two-day "moon," as Missy called their honeymoon, in the bridal suite at the Grove Park Inn. They had the rest of their lives to be together. Both were eager to make every day a honeymoon and begin their lives as parents to Missy.

There was no more beautiful place than western North Carolina, they agreed as they drove on the parkway toward the inn and stopped at an overlook.

"Missy would love this," Richard said.

"Stop worrying, Richard. Missy will look forward to the huge teddy bear you promised her. She'll get over being disappointed about not coming on the honeymoon with us. And she'll understand it in about ten years or so."

Richard grimaced. "In the meantime, I have to live with her. Try and keep two women happy."

Ellen grinned. "Two or more."

He drew her close. "The more the merrier. I can picture you now. That yellow canary singing to the little ones."

She nodded. "While daddy goes out and gets worms."

He laughed. "I'm the lion, remember." He grew serious. "You and Missy and your dad, Daisy too, are part of my territory now, Ellen." He took a deep breath and exhaled. "I don't want to keep bringing it up, but let me say this. I'll probably think of my past many times—particularly if and when you get pregnant. But it's not like an albatross around my neck anymore. It's a fact. One I accept. One I forgive myself for. I know it wasn't intentional, although it involved my own selfishness."

"It also involved your fear, Richard. You were a young man with dreams. With plans and goals. You saw that tumbling down. You saw yourself as a failure before you even got started."

"Dreams change."

"Yes, Richard. I didn't dream of you." She grinned. "Until after I met you. And now I feel my dreams are coming true. Spending my life with you, finding the mate God intended for me. That's more important than a job."

"I'm glad to hear you say that. I'll quit my job, and we'll live on love."

Ellen poked him on the arm lightly with her fist. He drew her to him, held her tightly, and kissed her. When they broke away, he kept his arm around her waist.

The pastor had pronounced that Ellen was his "to have and to hold" from that moment forward. Richard was holding her. . .in his heart.

Ellen looked up at him and said gently, "Richard, you don't want to keep talking about it, but don't you think your little baby is in heaven with God and Jesus, clapping her hands that you're no longer worrying about her?"

He inhaled deeply. "I like that picture. Before, I've thought of her wanting to ask me why I didn't want her. Why I didn't let her have a life on earth." He glanced around quickly, surprised. "Do you realize you said her?"

"I don't know why," Ellen said. "I just pictured a little girl. Maybe because of Missy."

Richard smiled. "I've always thought of her as a girl. You've done so much for me, Ellen. I believe God brought you to me for many reasons."

"Well, if I've done my job, I'll leave." She turned to walk away.

Richard caught her arm, and she didn't resist when he brought her back to him. "Oh no, you don't. It will take you a lifetime to straighten me out."

"I welcome the challenge," she said and snuggled closer to him. This was the beginning of their life together.

"Let's just stand here a moment and enjoy God's great creation."

Ellen looked out over the miles and miles of lush green forests. How far she had come from that stormy day when her life was at such a low point. How true that God's mysterious ways could take one from the valleys of life and set them on the mountaintops.

And today was particularly awe-inspiring. Sometimes clouds or fog obscured the view. Not today.

"It's so clear," Ellen said.

"And for the first time, in a long time," Richard said. "I feel clear-headed."

She looked up at him. "You know what they say about a clear day?"

"Yes." Richard glanced up at the blue sky, imagining a happy little girl with curls bouncing as she danced and sang and clapped her hands. Then he thought of one entrusted to him to nurture, along with her beautiful mother. He drew Ellen close.

"Yes. On a clear day, you can see forever."

A Letter To Our Readers

Dear Reader:

In order that we might better contribute to your reading enjoyment, we would appreciate your taking a few minutes to respond to the following questions. We welcome your comments and read each form and letter we receive. When completed, please return to the following:

Fiction Editor
Heartsong Presents
PO Box 719
Uhrichsville, Ohio 44683

1. Did you enjoy reading *On a Clear Day* by Yvonne Lehman?
   ❏ Very much! I would like to see more books by this author!
   ❏ Moderately. I would have enjoyed it more if

   _____

   _____

   _____

2. Are you a member of **Heartsong Presents**?   ❏ Yes   ❏ No
   If no, where did you purchase this book? _____

   _____

3. How would you rate, on a scale from 1 (poor) to 5 (superior), the cover design? _____

4. On a scale from 1 (poor) to 10 (superior), please rate the following elements.

   ____ Heroine   ____ Plot
   ____ Hero   ____ Inspirational theme
   ____ Setting   ____ Secondary characters

5. These characters were special because?_____
_____
_____

6. How has this book inspired your life?_____
_____
_____

7. What settings would you like to see covered in future
   Heartsong Presents books? _____
_____
_____

8. What are some inspirational themes you would like to see
   treated in future books? _____
_____
_____

9. Would you be interested in reading other **Heartsong
   Presents** titles? ❏ Yes ❏ No

10. Please check your age range:
    ❏ Under 18   ❏ 18-24
    ❏ 25-34   ❏ 35-45
    ❏ 46-55   ❏ Over 55

Name_____
Occupation _____
Address _____
City_____ State_____ Zip_____

Minnesota

*I*n 1877, the citizens of Chippewa Falls, Minnesota, are recovering from the devastation of a five-year grasshopper infestation. Throughout the years that follow, countless hardships, trials, and life-threatening dangers will plague the settlers as they struggle for survival amidst the harsh environs and crude conditions of the state's southwest plains. Yet love always prevails.

Historical, paperback, 480 pages, 5 ³/₁₆" x 8"

♥ • ♥ • ♥ • ♥ • ♥ • ❤ • ♥ • ♥ • ♥ • ♥ • ♥

♥ • ♥ • ♥ • ♥ • ♥ • ❤ • ♥ • ♥ • ♥ • ♥ • ♥

Heart♥ng

HEARTSONG PRESENTS TITLES AVAILABLE NOW:

Presents

$\mathcal{H}$EARTSONG ❤ PRESENTS

Love Stories Are Rated G!

That's for godly, gratifying, and of course, great! If you love a thrilling love story but don't appreciate the sordidness of some popular paperback romances, **Heartsong Presents** is for you. In fact, **Heartsong Presents** is the only inspirational romance book club featuring love stories where Christian faith is the primary ingredient in a marriage relationship.

Sign up today to receive your first set of four, never-before-published Christian romances. Send no money now; you will receive a bill with the first shipment. You may cancel at any time without obligation, and if you aren't completely satisfied with any selection, you may return the books for an immediate refund!

Imagine. . .four new romances every four weeks—two historical, two contemporary—with men and women like you who long to meet the one God has chosen as the love of their lives. . .all for the low price of $10.99 postpaid.

To join, simply complete the coupon below and mail to the address provided. **Heartsong Presents** romances are rated G for another reason: They'll arrive Godspeed!

YES! Sign me up for Hearts ❤ng!

NEW MEMBERSHIPS WILL BE SHIPPED IMMEDIATELY!
Send no money now. We'll bill you only $10.99 post-paid with your first shipment of four books. Or for faster action, call toll free 1-800-847-8270.

NAME _____

ADDRESS _____

CITY _____ STATE _____ ZIP _____

MAIL TO: HEARTSONG PRESENTS, P.O. Box 721, Uhrichsville, Ohio 44683
or visit www.heartsongpresents.com